Books Published by Black Freighter Productions
(BFP Books)

*C.R.I.M.E: Replacing Violence with
Compassion, Respect, Inspiration, Motivation, and Empathy*
by the Stand Up! Help Out! C.R.I.M.E. Teens
and Jeffrey J. Bulanda, Ph.D. and Rachel Kibblesmith, M.S.W.

*Onboarding: A Flightplan for Taking
Your Workforce to New Heights*
by Gia Suggs, Ed.D.

Suluhu
by the Stand Up! Help Out! C.R.I.M.E. Teens
and Katherine Tyson McCrea, Ph.D.

Cold Sweat
by Camil Williams

Poetic Hustles Anthology

Moral Horror Anthology

Traces

Solomohn Ennis-Klyczek
Foreword by Dr. Carl C. Bell, M.D.

bfpbooks.biz

Black Freighter Productions (BFP Books)
www.bfpbooks.biz

Traces © 2016 by Solomohn Ennis-Klyczek

First Edition: May 2016
Printed in the United States of America

ISBN 13: 978-0-9801114-2-2
Library of Congress Cataloging-in-Publication: 2016902505

Traces is an inspired work of fiction. All characters and events are products of the author's imagination that were inspired by real events and/or people.

Editor:
John Adam Klyczek
Cover image credit:
Ysbrand Cosijn
Author's image credit:
Terri Coleman

For my brothers and sisters *(of every faith, complexion, and persuasion)* who are committed to the struggle of overcoming strongholds caused by sexual trauma and an unregulated thought life.

Foreword

Whenever I am asked to write an endorsement of a work of art, I always have some mild concern. Although, I study the sometimes very murky scientific discipline of psychiatry, I still consider myself a scientist; ergo, I am mostly concerned with scientific proof and facts. When I was asked to review and possibly endorse *Traces,* a "Christian horror story," I was both cautious and solicitous about the request. The work is described by the author, Solomohn Ennis-Klyczek, as a book intended for people who have been sexually abused and those who are in the web of being a victim and a person who victimizes. I figured, if nothing else, I'll make sure the author is being accurate about her portrayal of this common problem in society.

Based on my clinical experience and scientific research, it is extraordinarily clear to me that many anxiety disorders stem from childhood trauma, most notable childhood sexual abuse. However, the all too common problem of sexual abuse of children is rarely discussed in polite society, and I think this is due to shame, guilt, fear, denial, and other emotional and psychological reasons for keeping this problem in the dark.

It is estimated that one in ten children are sexually abused. Having practiced psychiatry for nearly half a century, victims of childhood sexual abuse frequently consult me to help them heal their psychological, emotional and spiritual wounds. Typically, they are suffering from low self-esteem and symptoms of anxiety that are directly correlated with their history of childhood sexual abuse and its various resulting traumas; remarkably, *Traces* addresses these issues in a tasteful and genuine manner.

As a reader, who is entirely committed to helping others, I was immediately drawn into the world of the main character, Oakland, a mental health counselor in search of resolution for his own trauma, which includes childhood sexual abuse. Interestingly, through his experience, the potential risk for engaging in victimizing as a result of having been victimized is exposed, but it is balanced with Christian messages of discipline and salvation.

Personally, I have often sensed that church is a trauma magnet and that many of the parishioners are seeking to be "born again" as a way to *not* let their trauma define them. Unfortunately, *unlike* this book, my experience is that most churches refuse to encourage exposure of childhood sexual assault as a source of childhood trauma; it is easier to talk about being saved from drug abuse or homelessness or a life of crime, but childhood sexual abuse is almost just too much to put on the table in a religious context.

In contrast, *Traces* openly examines common outcomes associated with childhood sexual abuse delicately and authentically. As a work of fiction, *Traces* goes directly and straight to the heart of the matter; it is a welcomed addition to efforts that are purposed for highlighting risk factors and are directed toward providing protective factors for the treatment of childhood sexual abuse from a Christian perspective.

Dr. Carl C. Bell, M.D., D.L.F.A.P.A., F.A.C. Psych.

Dr. Carl C. Bell, M.D. is currently working with one of Illinois' most vulnerable and underserved populations as a staff psychiatrist at Jackson Park Hospital. Dr. Bell is a Distinguished Life Fellow of the American Psychiatric Association; he is a Fellow of the American College of Psychiatrist; he is retired from his position as President and Chief Executive Officer at the Community Mental Health Council, Inc.; he is retired from his position as Director of the Institute for Juvenile Research, which is the birthplace of Child Psychiatry; also, he is retired from his position as a Professor at the University of Illinois at Chicago's School of Public Health and Psychiatric Institute.

Preface

Working from the axiom that hurting people hurt people, it is with great fear and concern for the well-being of society, our children, and the adults and young adults who commit sexual crimes (specifically, against children) that *Traces* was conceived.

According to published reports by narrative therapists and cognitive literary studies researchers, "we form relationships with narrative[s]" (Wojciehowski and Gallese 2; Carr). Thus, the act of reading has been proven to have the ability to influentially engage the imagination to the extent that the material being consumed shapes our worldview, feelings, and thoughts about self. As a narrative, *Traces* affords its readers moments of psychological and emotional reflection and respite; in hopes that, those moments will bridge gaps that have obstructed the building of healthier, life-affirming schemas.

The characters and plot of *Traces* are based on years of research, and personal experiences. Authenticity and sincerity are especially important components of *Traces* because believability, and emotional and intellectual commonality are essential to the forming of the reader/narrative relationship. *Traces* has been purposed and designed to allow readers an escape into a text world that is similar enough to be familiar, different enough to remain interesting, and relevant enough to inspire change.

It is hoped that the textworld of *Traces* will free up mental space, create distance, and allow for objectivity as readers ponder the lives and circumstances of its characters, and that all of this combined will lead to an inspired reading and literary moment in which the reader can engage in identifying destructive behaviors and modes of thinking, and become active agents in their own recovery, habilitation, and re-authoring.

To prompt a significant response in readers, supernatural and spiritual elements of Christian-based faiths have been incorporated into *Traces*. As a Christian myself, I am a staunch believer in the power Christ has to completely re-wire spiritual and behavioral strongholds, so I paired Christianity with horror because the fear of hell and the desire for heaven have been known to be great motivators when correcting lifestyles. Furthermore, horror provides a narrative arc that supports discovery, confirmation, and confrontation, which are all vital steps in changing behavior. Art-Horror Theorist Noël Carroll states that, "…horror is an emotion…that horror narratives are designed to elicit…" (24). Being as such, it is my wish that *Traces* will horrify its readers into a blessed state of repentance and change.

To be clear, the horror in *Traces* is not gore; it's psychological, situational, morally-based. It's not monsters jumping from the pages, it's monsters (demons) controlling characters' lives. To fully experience it, the reader has to put self into the shoes of the character, embody concerns and motivations, and imagine being bound to regrets, deadly desires, and inescapable consequences. The horror in *Traces* is about the wages of sin and the interim payments of those sins being remitted to the demons of hell.

Solomohn Ennis-Klyczek, M.S., M.A.

Research cited:

"Adverse Childhood Experiences Study: Data and Statistics" published by the Atlanta Centers for Disease Control and Prevention for the National Center for Injury Prevention and Control in 2005.

"How Stories Make Us Feel: Toward an Embodied Narratology" written by Gallese Vittorio and Hannah Wojciehowski, published in *California Italian Studies Journal* in 2011.

"Michael White's Narrative Therapy" written by Alan Carr, published in the *Contemporary Family Therapy* journal in 1998.

"Sexual Victimization Reported by Former State Prisoners, 2008" published by the Bureau of Justice Statistics in 2012.

The Philosophy of Horror written by Noël Carroll, published by Routledge in 1990.

Abuse scenes:

The use of graphic sexual descriptions and vulgar language have been **avoided** in this text. However, there are still a few scenes that may be possible triggers for some people (the characters and page numbers are listed):

Oakland and man at playground, pp. 88-89

Queena, Jaymel, and Uncle Dakari, pp. 90-91

Baby Eddie and Trais, pp. 109-111

Girl on bus and Trais, pp. 110-111

Key *Bible* scriptures:

Deuteronomy 5:9, p. 30: "For I, the Lord your God, am a jealous God, visiting the iniquity of the fathers upon the children to the third and fourth generations of those who hate Me...".

Deuteronomy 24:16, p. 31: "Fathers shall not be put to death for their children, nor shall children be put to death for their fathers; a person shall be put to death for his own sin."

Ephesians 6:12, p. 44: "For we do not wrestle against flesh and blood, but against principalities, against powers, against the rulers of the darkness of this age, against spiritual hosts of wickedness in the heavenly places."

Numbers 22:28, p. 72: "Then the Lord opened the mouth of the donkey, and she said to Balaam, 'What have I done to you, that you have struck me these three times?'"

Colossians 1:16, p. 72: "For by Him all things were created that are in heaven and that are on earth, visible and invisible, whether thrones or dominions or principalities or powers. All things were created through Him and for Him."

John 1:3, p. 72: "All things were made through Him, and without Him nothing was made that was made."

1 John 4:4, p. 84: "You are of God, little children, and have overcome them, because He who is in you is greater than he who is in the world."

Deuteronomy 18:10-11, p. 82: "There shall not be found among you any one that maketh his son or his daughter to pass through the fire, or that useth divination, or an observer of times, or an enchanter, or a witch. Or a charmer, or a consulter with familiar spirits, or a wizard, or a necromancer."

Job 13:15, p. 92: "Though He slay me, yet will I trust in Him. Blessed be the name of the Lord."

Matthew 12:43-45, p. 95: "When an impure spirit comes out of a person, it goes through arid places seeking rest and does not find it. Then it says, 'I will return to the house I left.' When it arrives, it finds the house unoccupied, swept clean and put in order. Then it goes and takes with it seven other spirits more wicked than itself, and they go in and live there. And the final condition of that person is worse than the first. That is how it will be with this wicked generation."

2 Corinthians 5:14, p. 95: "For Christ's love compels us, because we are convinced that one died for all, and therefore all died."

2 Peter 3:8, p. 97: "But do not forget this one thing, dear friends: With the Lord a day is like a thousand years, and a thousand years are like a day."

Matthew 7:7-8, p. 138: "Ask, and it will be given to you; seek, and you will find; knock, and it will be opened to you. For everyone who asks receives, and he who seeks finds, and to him who knocks it will be opened."

Matthew 18:6, p. 139: "Whoever causes one of these little ones who believe in Me to sin, it would be better for him if a millstone were hung around his neck, and he were drowned in the depth of the sea."

Part One
The Awakening

1

The story was heart-wrenching. Oakland McCall had been working sixty hours a week for the last month, so he had only heard bits and pieces here and there about a real-life tragedy that upset every person unfortunate enough to hear about it.

The entire southern Illinois region had been rocked by the case. It was so disturbing that even Chicago and other nationally distributed newspapers picked it up. Oakland could not walk into any business, gas station, or restaurant in the relaxed, townsy city of Carbondale, Illinois, without overhearing someone talking about the investigation.

Before now, Oakland had been too busy to pay attention to what else was going on in the world. However, at this moment, he was stuck in his dentist's office.

Dr. Chloe's office is not typical; on most days, it is filled wall-to-wall with chatty local sharing their personal stories and opinions, making it feel more like a barber shop or beauty salon. Sometimes even Dr. Chloe would take her lunch up front and sit by the water station and talk and laugh as if she was waiting to be examined.

Consequently, on this day, there was nothing jovial about the atmosphere or the topic being discussed. Everyone in the office was somberly vocalizing what they had heard, read, or seen, and was trying to make sense of it all.

At the receptionist desk, Michele, the secretary, was talking to a pharmaceutical salesperson rather passionately about the young boy who had been molested in the nearby town of Anna. Her large, coarse cluster of coils glistened with each turn of her head. She said to the young blonde, "Paige, you know, many of our clients are from there. Everyone is outraged. They say this tragedy has brought all those that were divided together."

Immediately, a hefty, pale, woman with long dark hair and an "I Heart Giant City State Park" hat on chimed in. She said, "The one good thing about all this here terribleness is, honey, it done laid waste to the thangs that divided everybody. Black/White issues, male/female, Christian/Muslim, not nobody gives two darns about any of that right now." She closed her statement with a humph, then went back to reading a copy of the *Guideposts* magazines that Dr. Chloe displayed in every magazine stand and on every coffee table in the waiting area.

Oakland, having traveled through Anna, was intrigued by the racial unity the women spoke of. Anna was uncomfortable to him when he worked there ten years ago. It had been a sundown town many decades before; however, nearly a half-century later, for a considerable amount of the population the old feelings lingered. So, Oakland knew the gravity of the women's statements, and because he had heard in passing that the victim's family was Black this information really piqued his interest.

Across from Oakland, a melodic voice pulled at his attention. A woman with a T-shirt that read "Poetry is My Life" was conversing with two other women. She said to them, "When the Redding family cried out from their souls pleading for anyone to help them find who molested their son, if you possessed even the faintest ideas about love and compassion you could not help but shed a tear."

By this time, everyone in the waiting area was expressing how the case was affecting the people of Anna.

Near the office's entrance, a ruddy, long beard, muddy boots, young White man with Midwestern cowboy flair talked to a SIUC-sweatshirt wearing young Latino man. He said to him, "You know Joe Jenkins?"

University said, "The metalsmith? The Black guy?"

"Yeah," Ruddy said, "You remember Jeter Baker?"

University said, "That lumberjack white dude?"

"Emmhmm" Ruddy said, "You know they been going at it since we was young'ns. Even they said they'd work together to strang up the lowlife that touched Baby Eddie."

Just as the words "strang up" were forming an image in Oakland's mind, his name was called.

Dr. Chloe stood at the opened door that separated the waiting area from the examination rooms. She welcomed him kindly, but her eyes did not meet his as they typically do. As he walked toward her, he noticed she was looking behind and around him, and was deeply engrossed in the conversations being busily discussed in the waiting area of her office.

2

Though Dr. Chloe's handshake was firm, neither her eyes nor her smile possessed the same strength. Without any uncertainty, Oakland knew that something had gotten the best of his known to be strong, pleasant, and engaging doctor. Never before had he seen her reserved, or heard her voice softened to that of a loud whisper. As they walked down the hall of her spotless clinic and into the sanitized exam area that smelled of cleaning products and lilacs, Oakland noticed a sag in his doctor's typically straight, broad shoulders.

Moments after she closed the door, and both settled into their respective seats, Oakland thought about how it was Dr. Chloe who had given him, as a Christmas gift to all of her clients that year, copies of *Beloved* and *Who Switched Off My Brain?*

Oakland also remembered that it was Dr. Chloe who he could count on to discuss the most painful human experiences thoughtfully and introspectively without pretense. She called it discussing "'the size of human life.'"

And, Dr. Chloe was also the first person who candidly talked to Oakland about examining his past critically. She would say, "'The past has a life of its own.' It's always showing up in the present. You gotta be aware of it. It can motivate you to do things, think things, be things without even the faintest bit of awareness from your present self."

In this moment, Oakland was recalling when he cried, in the very chair he was sitting in. It wasn't long ago. One of Oakland's clients had landed in jail because he refused to fight against desires that had been instilled in him during his youth. Being a seasoned mental health counselor who had worked in various sex offender treatment programs, the situation should not have bothered Oakland so deeply, but it did. During his career, Oakland had treated men, women, juveniles, who had awful things done to them and had done awful things to others. But, it was something about the Foster case that brought Oakland a restless sorrow. It was look in his client's eyes when he said, "Something happened to me. Something I can't fully remember, but keep acting on. I'm not sure, but I feel like it's behind what I've become." Oakland wrestled with the words after leaving the client and all the way to Dr. Chloe's office. He wasn't in Dr. Chloe's chair two minutes before the tears started falling and would not stop.

Even then, busy as she was, Dr. Chloe prayed with him about the client, and talked with him about similar stories she had heard throughout the years involving her family members and those of others who, as she put it, "thought themselves into the actions of a reprobate mind."

Sitting in Dr. Chloe's chair today, Oakland waited until after they had a few niceties and check-up questions before asking his known to be conscientious and critical thinking dentist, "Concerning that case that's all over the news, why, out of all the crimes that happen every day, to all the people they happen to, are people taking such special interest in this case?"

Dr. Chloe wheeled back on her stool. She looked at Oakland's yellow-brown complexion, his perfectly razored crew cut, the sleeves of his starched shirt, the cuffs of his tailored slacks, and the high shine of his calfskin shoes. She asked him, "Do you know the child or his family?"

Oakland surmised that something about his style of dress and the way he carries himself led her to ask. He said to her, "No. Should I?"

Dr. Chloe with an audible sigh said, "Well, I do. And possibly you should too." She wheeled back toward him before she continued, "Anyway, I know you know the racial climate in Anna because we've talked about it before. And I can tell you, all the hoopla is not because the little boy is Black neither is it about the family being well-respected."

Before Dr. Chloe could continue, her white lab coat pocket glowed. Uncustomarily, she actually looked at her phone. She swiped the screen several times, quickly scanned whatever was on it, then shoved it back into her pocket while apologizing distractedly.

Oakland could tell by the faraway look on her face that she needed to be brought back into the moment, so he prompted her. He said, "Dr. Chloe, certainly there are reasons that cannot be explained—timing, the moon, the waves, who knows. But in your heart of hearts—since you know them—what's the deal? I mean, as a counselor, I'm glad to see everyone up in arms, specifically, about this type of a crime. I wish every case received such a response from the community. People are really moved by this one."

Dr. Chloe adjusted the computerized chair Oakland sat in, then said, "The boy who was molested, he is the sweetest, kindest, most gentle boy I've ever known. Oakland, you know I can be a very practical person, very much about the here and now, the explainable. But that boy, I know in my soul, he's an angel. And everyone who's met him or been around him agrees."

Oakland looked at Dr. Chloe perplexedly. To hear her say those words with the same conviction she uses when explaining why flossing and brushing daily is mandatory made him take especial notice.

"Seriously, Oakland," she said, "we've all talked about it. For example, I've been out with the family at times, and the most racist, life-hating Whites seem to hate a little less in his presence. Same thing with the Blacks, even the most self-loathing Blacks, their energy becomes noticeably gentle when he is around. I know that boy's blessedness firsthand."

Oakland took in what she said. He looked at her natty gray hair, her skin which was the color of a Brazil nut's shell, and knew she knew firsthand about the special kind of hate that people hurl at others who are different than themselves. To prevent the pains that each of them carried as Black people who have been subjected to colorism and racism, Oakland moved forward with the subject, "So what about the perp?"

"Oh, Oakland," Dr. Chloe said, "that's the latest development. I just received it on my feed. Based on what just popped up, he was killed yesterday in Chicago. He was beaten to death." Dr. Chloe paused for a moment to adjust the lamp and fit her gloves onto her hands. She continued, "I haven't had an opportunity to read the entire story yet. But from what I could see, he was a young, Black boy, seventeen years old. It's a shame he was already so disturbed. His name was Trais Johnson."

The reality of that statement caused both of them to inhale deeply. Thinking as a clinician, Oakland was further disturbed by the young man's overtly opportunistic predatory behavior. As Dr. Chloe checked his teeth, Oakland thought about all of the possibilities, all the conclusions people would draw, and how current stigmas would be hyper-inflated, and how all of it together would be yet another weight to carry for the young Black men who were in any way associated with or similar to Trais Johnson's identity.

As soon as Dr. Chloe removed the retractor from Oakland's mouth, he wasted no time recalling how all his life he had been grouped into one stereotype or the other, and how most often people would characterize him based on whatever negative portrayal the local news stations were broadcasting. Oakland immediately began reminding Dr. Chloe of the prevalence of sexual crimes and the ones they'd discussed over the years.

With an exactness sharpened by decades of diligent study and intense observations, Oakland explained, "I've found one thing that's consistent amongst people who commit sexual crimes. From textbooks to practice, regardless of their age, race, class, sexual preference, or gender—each one of 'em—all of 'em had a grossly unregulated thought life."

In response to what Oakland said, Dr. Chloe pursed her lips and shook her head in dismal agreement.

Oakland continued, "And you know what else, their thought life becomes a stronghold like none I've ever seen either. It truly is an evil spirit that grows within them, specifically in that area of their lives that wants for intimacy and touch, and from there it festers; that demonic force takes hold of them and feeds on their destruction of self and others. That's why, with sex crimes, you can't just concentrate on the crime or just that one facet of the person; you have to look at everything-the seen and the unseen."

Dr. Chloe knew about the all-consuming power of spiritual strongholds better than most. However the closeness of this tragedy elicited double pity from her and produced big breathy sighs reserved for the unbelievably incomprehensible. After a few moments of reflection, she remembered something she read that stood out to her.

Dr. Chloe said to Oakland, "You know what was strange, you know strange for someone who'd go so far as to do what he did being as young as he was, a witness reported him saying that he was sorry and that he didn't want to be a pedophile. Now, what he said, and what you just said got me thinking, what was really motivating that young man? I can certainly see it being bio, psycho, social and cultural influences, but I can also see it being more than that, you know an evil spirit, specifically one that comes to kill, steal and destroy."

Oakland processed Dr. Chloe's logic as she busied herself preparing the room for her next patient. He began thinking about the young man's actions, not just in terms of their spiritual origins, but also within the context of what Dr. Chloe mentioned.

Then he thought about the young man being Black. And because of how the case was covered, and the lack of hearing otherwise, Oakland figured he was possibly poor too. He thought about what he knew of affordable mental health care in Chicago and how it was diminishing, and how it had just about dried up altogether for those living at, near, or beneath the poverty line.

As a professional, he pondered the providers he would have trusted to actually care for a young, poor, Black man. And he could only think of one, one who he knew would treat him with the level of conscientiousness and care necessary to treat chronic problems that caused certain danger—Dr. Meharry Compton. Because Meharry understood the value of meditation, exercise, a constructive disciplined thought life, and a lifestyle that promoted being of service to others in a way that benefited them without tearing them down, Oakland trusted him more than most.

Oakland sighed again when he remembered that even Compton's clinics had been negatively impacted by state-level fiscal woes. *Hmm*, Oakland thought, *yet another obstacle in a world filled with too many unnecessary disadvantages.*

Oakland placed his hand over his heart when he thought about the prospects for young Black males who struggle with mental challenges, and he nearly audibly whimpered when he thought about the most likely outcome for those who are also battling compulsive sexually deviant behavior. Oakland shook his head at the bleakness of the situation.

Dr. Chloe took his gesture as a response to her statement and decided to continue; she said with sincere pity, "I may be wrong but I can't help but think about all the help out here, especially for the youth. If you ask me, he didn't have to be the way he was." She paused for a moment to give what she said a second, not so idealistic thought, then shifted gears. "Well, maybe there isn't as much help as I think. Like I said, I haven't had a chance to read the entire story, maybe knowing more about him and his life will make it all make sense."

Ruminating on Dr. Chloe thinking that so much help was available and knowing that that was completely untrue made Oakland feel weak. So weak that he did not even have energy to correct her. Instead, he thanked his doctor kindly and left from her sight with a wave.

As he neared the exit, he could hear people talking about the latest news about Trais Johnson. In that moment, Oakland decided that he would take some time away from work to see what he could learn about this tragically flawed, spiritually troubled young man.

3

Immediately after leaving Dr. Chloe's office, Oakland picked up some local and regional papers at a gas station. His favorite hangout, Southern Illinois University, with its fine arts and community events, held much promise for an enjoyable Friday night. However, being compelled to learn more about Trais Johnson, Oakland continued past SIU's attractions and journeyed home.

At his house, not far from the university's backyard, Oakland thumbed through the newspapers, visited websites, and listened to podcasts. When he happened upon one particular paper with an especially clear image of the young man's face, he closed and opened it several times. So striking were Trais Johnson's features, Oakland decided he needed to zoom in. *My goodness,* Oakland thought to himself, *this young man looks exactly like me.* Hurriedly, he punched up the story on his tablet. Right there in the clearest pixels money could buy, Oakland saw an exact copy of his very own eyes, nose and mouth.

Oakland's mind began counting, thinking back, remembering. It had been exactly eighteen years since he left Chicago. Oakland thought about it, 350 miles were between him and where he grew up, where he had his first kiss, fell for his first love, and now 350 miles marked the distance between where an exact copy of his eyes, nose, and mouth had lain dead in the street.

All of this rightly troubled Oakland. He paced his floors, made himself some tea. He sat down. He stood up. He turned the lights on, opened the curtains, looked in the big mirror he kept in the hall, and placed Trais's magnified image right side his own living breathing face. The more he looked, the more they looked alike. His knees felt weak. He started sweating. *Lord, have mercy,* he thought.

He had to get some rest. Very much unlike his daily routine, he took a nap at two in the afternoon. "Some sleep will calm me and help me get a more logical perspective," he told himself.

After two dreamless nights, his heart was still racing. After five naps stretched out over the course of many hours, his house, his very own house all at once looked unfamiliar, and his face, his face seemed more like Trais's than his own.

After an entire weekend filled with comparisons and contrasts and correlations, Oakland finally gave in to doing some serious thinking back, some remembering with purpose.

That Sunday afternoon, he sat at his dining room table and made himself a time line so that he could chart the events of his own life. Beneath the time line, he made space for naming emotions, people, and places. While looking at the blank diagram, Oakland made a declaration. He said aloud, "I'll do what I've asked all of my clients to do, be brave and honest while looking at the past." Then, he put pencil to paper and began the process of filling-in the empty spaces.

4

Not long after Oakland began writing, it occurred to him that it was not just Trais's face that was interrupting the regular flow of his life; his partially filled-in chart had already uncovered events and relationships that long troubled him, but had not been actively thought of for many years.

Since before the time Oakland was a young airman, at the age of eighteen, serving his country in Lajes Field, Azores, every now and again he'd have a paternal sensation-a feeling that he was connected to something, someone in a fatherly way. On and off over the years, he'd catch himself thinking about being a parent, not longing to be a father, but actually being one. Especially in the month of November, the thoughts and feelings would slip past reality, as he knew it, and make themselves known.

When visiting family for the holidays, they would complain about him talking loudly while sleeping. They'd tease him, "Oakland, you sure you ain't got no kids? All that 'my son, my son' talk in your sleep says otherwise."

Oakland would just laugh it off. He had heard similar observations from different people at different times over the years. However, he was so distanced from his own true feelings about what was being said that he never allowed himself to feel bothered by it enough to fathom that the possibility even existed.

Thinking about it now, Oakland figured the way he'd been handling his sleep talking and fatherly inclinations was no coincidence.

Since childhood, he had been conditioned to not be the sort of person who would speak of anything he was unsure about. His silence about the intangible and anything he did not have first-hand knowledge of was a habit seared into his being by his mother and siblings. Their meanness imposed upon him an unnatural tendency to not think aloud, to avoid wondering, or casually discussing his ideas.

As a child, Oakland had been relegated to only speaking when spoken to and feeling like anything about his life was not important or interesting enough to share. By the time he was seven, only his imaginary friend and grandmother knew anything of his opinionated and observant nature. Though harmful, all of the silent treatment and honed ability to keep to one's self had its benefits.

At about the age of eight, Oakland began demonstrating strictness over his social interactions. He possessed an external control amongst others that exceeded his years. When he did speak, he demonstrated maturity, which made him the love supreme of his fastidious grandmother.

Oakland's grandmother, Hassie, would say to Oakland's mom, who everybody referred to as Ms. Lucy, that, "This one, he's special. If you raise him up right, both of y'all will be blessed."

Ms. Lucy, although pleased to hear such words from her mother, couldn't help but be broken-hearted. Her mother had not said the same about her or her other children. And for that oversight, Ms. Lucy neglected Oakland.

Ms. Lucy's heart was once soft heart, but it had grown ornery due to a lack of validation and affection in her own life; in turn, she only gave Oakland, in particular, so much love. Since her mama was head over heels for her middle child, she figured that he "with all his smartness" could get the love he needed from her.

In reaction to Ms. Lucy's orneriness, Hassie heaped praise upon her grandbaby for his self-control and his "unlike his mamaness" in the form of lessons in the arts, music, spirituality, and culture.

For people of their status and class, lessons in culture came from unlikely sources. Hassie pulled every string and tapped the shoulder of every well-to-do person she came in contact with to enrich the life of her grandson. Hassie's savviness and forward-thinking paid off too. Taking her gorgeous, bright-eyed Oakland to open civic discussions and scholarly debates put both of them into contact with the Black intelligentsia of Chicago.

At the age of ten, he was spending hours upon hours at the DuSable Museum comparing and contrasting African and African-American cultures. At the DuSable, the vast varieties of those cultures and the many cultures within them were laid before him in the form of books, exhibits, and performances.

It was at the DuSable that the foundation of Oakland's predisposition for being actively engaged and seeking answers through books and most importantly through experiences became central to his learning process.

Hassie, honoring her grandson's earnest nature and curious mind, determined it would be good for Oakland to venture further from home. Although Hassie did not care much for her sisters' nomadic missionary lifestyle, she understood the value of their travels and ways of thinking. So every now and again, she'd petition his mother to allow Oakland to be sent on trips with her sisters as they traveled about the United States helping others in need.

While with his aunts, Iona and Angel, Oakland learned to appreciate different lifestyles, became more tolerant, and practiced open-mindedness, which his aunts always told him was most important. Although Oakland's immediate family were staunch Baptists with strict beliefs about holiness and the ways in which God communicates with his beloved, Iona and Angel helped all God's children regardless of how different their beliefs and faith practices were.

Whenever Oakland joined his aunts, the great-hearted women would welcome him with open arms. They loved Oakland and would sing songs of adoration to him. With his aunts, he learned to respect life in all its forms, regardless of culture, gender, or species.

Oakland also took a liking to animals, their interactions, the societies they formed and the hierarchies within those societies. He was amazed by the similarities animals had with humans, especially their motivations and emotions and behaviors that were related to food, shelter, social interactions, and jealousy.

After long days of learning what felt like everything that is good and important in life, his aunts would tuck Oakland in with moral tales filled with both the mercy and the wrath of God.

On one particular trip to a Pawnee reservation in Oklahoma, his aunts participated in a purification ceremony. That night, they had a shared dream, neither ever told another soul about what they saw, but they warned Hassie that something about the forces influencing Oakland disturbed them. Afterward, they took Oakland with them on a few more trips, but declined taking him away from home the year he became eleven.

During their last visit alone with Oakland, they prayed over him fervently and asked Jesus to protect him for all the days of his life. They also pleaded with Oakland to always give himself time to think through his actions, to seek wise counsel, to be mindful of his body, and not be overwhelmed by emotions.

At once, Oakland began feeling a connection between his aunts refusal of him and the confusion he began feeling shortly after they stopped taking him along.

He remembered that being an especially hard time because not only did he felt like he lost his two favorite aunts, but he also lost his cousins too. And, he was experiencing all types of changes with his body. He suddenly had this really intense and rather startling awareness about the physical differences between himself and other boys and men.

However the breaking point was when he overheard his cousins saying that they did not even want him to go to the park with them. That's when he had a bit of a breakdown. He ran to his aunt crying and pleading. He begged her to tell him what was wrong with them and why they didn't want to be with him.

Her response was odd. His aunt, Iona, took him to the side and told him about Deuteronomy 5:9, and how the iniquity of the father is visited upon the children. And, when he asked her what exactly she meant about the iniquity being visited. From that time until now, the expression on her face has haunted him. She sighed and said, "You will understand better than anyone can ever tell you in due time."

That was the last time Oakland saw his aunts and their children. And still, at this moment, her words caused Oakland all sorts of anxiety. He long let go of the pain he felt about his cousins because they ended up leading the types of lifestyles he wants nothing to do with; however, that scripture still bothered him, especially now.

To know that some spiritual problems started generations ago and had to be lived through to fulfill God's word and exact His judgment was frightening and struck him as unfair.

So, Oakland quickly opened his notes from his own personal times of devotion and another scripture caught his attention, Deuteronomy 24:16; it states, "Fathers shall not be put to death for their children, nor shall children be put to death for their fathers; a person shall be put to death for his own sin." The scripture quieted Oakland's fears. He rested in knowing that the trade-off for certain judgment was that God would give each person freedom and only hold His children responsible for the sins they committed as individuals. Though he wasn't fully sure why, 24:16 eased his mind enough to continue forward with his chart.

Still covering that period of his life, Oakland remembered how panic-stricken, deeply hurt and without recourse his eleven-year-old self felt because of his aunts' words and behavior. He also recalled that from the night she said that forward, he did the only thing his young mind could think to do and that was to neglect himself.

His mother and siblings did not value him, his aunts abandoned him, his father was there but not there, so he just started staying out of everyone's way, which eventually led him to silencing and ignoring his inner voice and instincts.

As a budding teenager, all of the ambiguity from some of his closest family members and ever-increasing the acidic attitude of his mother increased the potency of the hurt feelings he had about his now totally absentee father, and all of it combined began forming into a rather severe case of arrested development.

Though he excelled at all things academic and athletic, he had many personal hang-ups. By the time he was twelve, he had internalized the characteristics of what the kids at school called "weird."

As he developed into an actual teenager, he did not have the tools to grow out of the harsh inner-criticism that he had developed as a result of all the rejection, self-imposed and otherwise. By the time he was thirteen, the negativity culminated into a deep distrust of his own thought process and a heavy reliance upon validation from others.

And, that's when he met Tina; the pretty girl who lived near the school, who was always so nice to him, and would give him all kinds of goodies, and the attention that he desperately craved. It was February, and Oakland was fourteen. By Valentine's Day, he was in love. By March first, he found out she did not love him. It was a boom and bust relationship.

Tina left Oakland shortly after he started living and breathing for her. In her absence, nothing could console him; worst, on top of all his loneliness was his lost virginity; it was given to Tina. The one thing that all the kids at school were talking about—sex—Oakland had given it away, and now the person he gave it to wanted nothing to do with him, which made him feel even more rejected and wretched.

Within days, the love sickness that Tina left him with became a cancer. He evaluated any word that came from someone's mouth about him and appraised even the smallest of gestures. Any thing he felt was a sleight would make him question everything. And when he did not receive positive feedback, he would fall into deep zombie-like depressions.

He became unpredictable, moody, and nearly unbearable. The only person who could tolerate him and he was tolerable around was his grandmother. That tad of forced consistency with her is what kept him in contact with the only earthly joy he truly believed in. And when things got really bad, like really really bad, it was only his grandmother's love and prayers that gave him just enough strength and hope to not kill himself.

Although he was alive, for the most part, he was still suffering. Her love was enough to keep him going, but not enough to live in the type of light needed to cultivate a healthy self-awareness. And, inevitably, Oakland's lack of awareness in many areas of his life limited his view of his power and ultimately created a myriad of mental blocks.

Looking back on the darkness of his childhood, Oakland felt ever fortunate for the inheritance his grandmother left him on the eve of his sixteenth birthday, which was an arrangement for two years of Christian counseling; a well-worn *Holy Bible* and a prayer journal. The accompanying note written by her hand stated that he was to further his "edification" with the gifts, "never forget God's unchanging hand," and to "live holy" so that they could see one another again.

Oakland's counselor, knowing his grandmother's wishes, helped him identify and assess the effects his upbringing and humanity's fallen nature had on his inability to see himself as someone who could change outcomes, as someone who had power. The *Bible* and the journal, each in their own way, helped Oakland understand how to value life again, and to not be overly emotional about the inevitable suffering life brings.

As Oakland continued charting his experiences, it occurred to him that it was during that time in his life the seed of feeling valuable and powerful was planted, but it was not until his mid twenties that the ideas slowly began working their way into his daily life.

He also realized that it wasn't until after many years, much therapy, tireless self-introspection, and the building up of his mind and spirit that he began to access the kind of maturity necessary for consistent self-confidence.

Based on the details in his chart, it was while in graduate school that he began being aware of the purpose of his talents, and began valuing himself according to, not just his usefulness to others, but also the preciousness of his own life and how it in itself was an expression of God's love.

In this moment, the true value and connection between his grandmother's gift, his education, and his career choice became known to him. All of it together had given his life purpose and something worthwhile to think and do.

Oakland thought to himself, *I would not have become a counselor, let alone a Chris-*

tian counselor had it not been for my years with BJ. I bet grandma knew that. I bet grandma knew all of it, that's why she stepped in to help me.

Oakland was right again. All of the positive experiences Hassie had sacrificed greatly for were her good faith contributions to God that heaven would fulfill her prayer and urge Oakland toward a lifestyle and career that made all the wrong things right.

The truth is Oakland was blessed beyond measure for his observant grandmother. She knew something terrible had happened and was happening to him. She worried for Oakland without ceasing. She also saw the way Ms. Lucy treated him, and she knew he'd end up in the gutter like so many others if someone did not stop what they were doing and physically show him the light.

She'd study him in his frustration when he would be struggling with something. Things that had once been easy for him would be a struggle, that was the first sign. The second sign were the visible displays of hurt, powerlessness, disbelief in himself, and abnormal fear. Instead of shunning him, Hassie had mercy on him. It made the difference.

Instantly, Oakland felt gratitude for his life and abilities in a way that he had never felt before. However, in the very next moment that followed, Oakland felt great sadness for his clients, the many men and women and children, he had seen over the years who never reached such a level of self-actualization because no one ever paused long enough to show them the self in them that had been blinded and crippled by trauma.

Oakland also grieved for those who perpetuated their tragedies and remained captive to lifestyles that were forced upon them because they did not have the resources, had too much self-doubt, and were too utterly lost to free themselves.

It was within this mental space, while peering at Trais Johnson's face, that Oakland was pulled away from his typical thought patterns. Something about feeling fortunate, and really understanding how bad things could have been for him without his grandmother, refreshed his mind.

Oakland began thinking about himself as a rather accomplished survivor.

He had survived the emotional stinginess exacted upon him by his family as a child and still managed to become a caring, giving human being. He had pressed forward with his education though being in that setting was often times uncomfortable and triggered feelings from childhood of being harshly judged and disliked. He, despite all encumbrances, had become a responsible, principled, and kind man.

Looking at himself in this light gave Oakland a sense of power and opened his eyes to a kaleidoscope of possibilities. The process of charting and assessing his life rewarded him a breakthrough.

Oakland looked at Trais's image again, and he gave himself permission to think of himself as capable of making another human being.

For the first time in his life, Oakland brainstormed and clustered all the thoughts that had been categorized under miscellaneous and unthinkable. He allowed his mind to think logically.

He thought, *Did I get Tina pregnant? Do I have a son?* The idea in those explicit terms had been inconceivable before, but now with his renewed mind nothing could stop him from thinking it.

In a flash, uncertainty returned. Oakland thought, *Was it entirely my lack of self-confidence that prevented me from thinking I could have had a child?* He began thinking back yet again, then realized that he never once saw any signs of pregnancy.

He also recalled that he and Tina only had sex once, and that exactly one month after the relationship started she ended it. He remembered only seeing her once more before never seeing her again.

Six weeks after their break-up, he saw her on a bus. He was standing in the doorway of Mr. Bright's candy store when one of those big green CTA buses passed by. To this day, he still feels how it took everything inside of him not to drop his purchase and give chase.

Oakland wasn't sure if it was the distance from the memory, or the fact that he was not distracted by the pain of their separation, but right now he could recall something he never remembered consciously thinking before: Her face was puffy. Actually, Tina's face was noticeably heavier. Oakland slapped his own face with both palms. "She was pregnant," he exclaimed.

The decision was made. He knew he had to travel back to where he grew up. He had to find answers. He had to go back to where he came from.

Part Two

Discovery and Confirmation

5

Oakland could not help but feel the excitement of Chicago's downtown area as it came into view. At just a few moments after sunrise, on this perfectly pleasant breezy summer morning the traffic on Interstate 90/94 West was bumper to bumper and stop and go.

The wind was a just-right warm, so fellow drivers had their windows down and their volumes up. Some were listening to jazz, others talk radio, a few were tuned into classical music, and many were bopping to R&B, oldies, and techno sounds.

As Oakland exited the highway in his blue Tahoe and entered the city's crisscross of one-way streets, swarms of people were walking vigorously and moving about in every direction. Those who were stopped at the numerous intersections, waited impatiently, their legs twitched with anticipation. There were men and women in suits, delivery people, joggers, bicyclists, people playing instruments, and workers of every type seizing the day. Oakland thought as he looked into the quietness at the center of the chaos.

Despite all the bad news which all too often made its way to southern Illinois concerning the resource-sucking metropolis, on this July morning Chicago was a busy calm, living up to its motto "the city that works."

When Oakland pulled into the garage at Presidential Towers, he relished the quiet. He'd made arrangements with his good friend, Albeha, to leave his vehicle in her spot. With his car parked in the dark, isolated space, the worries began setting in.

He feared facing too much rejection, absentmindedness, or lack of concern from the people he would have to interact with to get what he needed. He imagined being dismissed and shuddered at how feeling unimportant would rattle the cage of dormant emotions barred back by time.

He envisioned sitting on a curb in his old neighborhood immobilized by awakened childhood hurts. Oakland knew he had to be calm, patient, and not be overwhelmed with feelings that would cause him to overreact, to do so could result in ending his mission prematurely, so as a practical precaution he allowed himself to mull over every terrible thing that could happen, then mentally pictured himself being victorious over all those things.

Twenty minutes later, he was walking the crowded streets headed for the Green Line train. Dresses in his gardening clothes, Oakland carried a plastic grocery bag, which held two bottles of water, a notepad, and a pencil, and in his pocket was a neatly folded article that had the clearest picture of Trais Johnson's face.

Oakland walked with purpose toward his destination and hummed, "Pass Me Not, Oh Gentle Savior." With each refrain his confidence and sense of destiny increased.

The train coasted and jolted, jolted and coasted on the rails of its elevated tracks. Between where he got on at Clinton and the current stop, Ashland, the clientele started to change. Before, people of all colors boarded and exited the train. They walked and talked and carried themselves with an air of importance. However, at California, the mix of colors began changing proportionately, and the overall mood became a rancid concoction of oppression made especially volatile by hostility. Making eye contact and smiling became "what you looking at?" So in order to avoid becoming the embodiment of some passenger's random frustration, Oakland turned his head and his attention toward the wide, clear windows of the train.

Looking down upon the landscape, he could see jalopies and luxury cars, and a variety of other markers that served as lines of delineation. In this area, just a few miles west of downtown Chicago, there were squares of ghettos within ghettos. Magnificent walk-up Greystones that were in disrepair yet holding their undeniable value bordered cheap tenements. Every now and again, here and there, all of it would be punctuated with properties that boasted recently repointed mortar joints, professional landscaping, and tightly sealed driveways. And inevitably the same mixes and matches he saw riding the train would be on the street, including both extremes and all of the spectrum in-between, each category of people would be most densely populated near their respective housing situation.

Oakland thought to himself, *Humph. I had heard but had never really noticed before, Chicago is quite segregated.*

Without warning the train halted. The people erupted into a chorus of expletives, and "I have to get to work ballads."

Over the loud speaker the conductor announced, "Sorry folks, I've been informed that there's a rather rowdy altercation down the way here. The police are en route. We'll getcha back moving shortly."

Oakland decided to keep his eyes glued out the window as the people agitatedly huffed and puffed behind him. With the train being stopped, he focused on the people walking the streets below. He saw Black men with bright bow ties, large mustaches, groomed beards and shoes that gleamed. Their blazers and vests fit them perfectly, and they were busy going in and out of a community center.

Oakland imagined they were the baton-running descendants of the upwardly mobile who marched with King and heeded the good word of Fred Hampton. As they passed out pamphlets and handed out fresh apples to passers-by, they had an uprightness about them that looked to never know shame or downheartedness. These people did not buy into the minority stereotype, they were the concentrated form of all that was productive, living what others only dared dream. They were the sons of the proletariat struggle. Oakland's instinct served him quite right because moments later a super sharp sister exited the building with an extra-large A-Frame sign that read: "All power to all people.

We work interminably for the right to political education, the right to civic power, and self-determination. We long for liberation. Come join us!"

Just as Oakland felt like standing up and shouting filled with the indomitable spirits of the Universal Negro Improvement Association, the American Civil Rights, and the Black Panther Party for Self-Defense movements, the train jerked forward and slow crawled the tracks.

The next scene he took in had equally dashing brothers and sisters but they were stepping over and stepping aside those who appeared less fortunate than them. Oakland knew this big smiles, sweaty hands bunch all too well. These were the sons and daughters of those who poured concrete over gardens, chased dollars, and lived as far away as they could from the neighborhoods they were wrecking.

They were the lowdown local powers, who were the yays of the quick loan businesses. It was them that rented their great grandmama's and granddaddy's buildings to people who poured acrylic over nails and sold liquor all night long; these were the vipers amongst the King-Hamptonites, the opportunists. Their motivations were selfish. Their community endeavors appeared helpful, but were actually exploitative. This particular crowd, they talked the talk, but their actions were self-serving.

They cared nothing about the people who paid for their services. Some of them were homegrown, some of them were implants. However, Oakland figured based on the abundance of "Sold" signs, many of them were well-off globetrotters who had meticulously calculated the area would undergo full-scale gentrification in the near future and wanted to get in while prices were still reasonable.

As the train crept closer and closer to Oakland's destination, he noticed how the well-kept and expensive was walkway-distance from dilapidated buildings, houses, and empty lots. Side-by-side they existed together, the extravagant and the much in need, the graffiti and the orchids, men who had never worked and men who had worked all their lives, and women who were leaders of industry and women whose children were being raised by the state.

The twenty-five-minute train ride finally positioned Oakland at Cicero and Lake, the epicenter of his old neighborhood. He wasn't sure if it was his thirty-two-year-old eyes or if he had just gotten use to the insulated middle-class life he'd been living in Carbondale, but this particular section of Chicago reminded him of Useni Eugene Perkins's book, *Home is a Dirty Street*. The unavoidable gang presence, the constant stream of squad cars, the boarded up houses, the overall trickle down cyclical lack of care, all of it was depressing in an enraging way.

Everything just looked like filth to him: It was not only the trash strewn from private property to public space, the misspelled vulgarities scribbled in spray paint across otherwise permissible exteriors, the drained malt liquor bottles laying on their sides in the gutter, the emptied baggies decorated with skulls and cannabis leaves that populated the sparse grassy areas like so many dandelions; it was also the food deserts, the flocks of homeless people, and the scores of abandoned buildings they stood in front of. It was overwhelming.

As he walked, Oakland could see that drug selling and prostitution did not stop on account of a Monday morning. All around him was a mess of juxtaposed contrasts. Some folks were undeniably under the influence and belligerently harassing children on their way to summer school. Others were taking it upon themselves to pick up trash and put it into bins. Along the way, a young pimp stood off in the distance keeping a vicious eye on even younger prostitutes. And catty-corner to them, a well-groomed teen-aged black boy and his three sisters stood at the bus stop practicing Swahili and looking cared for. Walking along the scum-encrusted sidewalks, Oakland was up close and personal with young men and women who had tracks on their arms, burnt lips, and blackened fingertips. While navigating intersections, he kept pace with young men and women with books under their arms discussing literature and talking about their plans for the future.

Moments later, he was arrested by an eerie feeling. It was as though he was passing through a field of energy, a portal of some kind. Desperate emotions coursed through his being, evil sensations surrounded him. The atmosphere was so awful, Oakland could not resist quickening his steps to that of a jog.

Still, the aura persisted, becoming more and more intense. Just as Oakland felt frightened enough to break out into a full run, something in his peripheral vision caught his eye.

A woman who was too old and a boy who was too young were looking way too comfortable with each other in the worst of ways. He scanned her appearance and memorized her tawny skin, pockmarked face, and opaque gray eyes, then at once the energy around him dissipated. It left as quickly as it came. Oakland stopped, blinked, rubbed his forehead then his face. The feeling had certainly passed. He looked back to see the woman and the child, but they were gone too. It all happened so rapidly, he wondered if it had happened at all.

As Oakland neared the corner, he waved at a group of men who looked to be from every continent on Earth. They were reminiscing about the first time they read Haki Madhubuti's *Don't Cry, Scream* and heard Nikki Giovanni and the New York Community Choir's "Like a Ripple on a Pond," and discussing the importance of art that inspires excellence.

Listening to them gave Oakland hope, but after moving through what felt like the valley of death, he still had to stop for a moment and rest a spell. As he looked about him from his seat on the park bench, he was astounded by the chaos, yet mesmerized by how everyone just kept on keeping on.

Recalling everything he'd seen up to this point, including some memories of Cicero and Lake from childhood, Oakland thought about how the faces had changed but much of what had been going on when he left was still going on now. Despite all of the improvements and advancements and all the other things that are supposed to change the world, Babylons and Gomorrahs still existed. All of it together led him to think that his quest to discover the who and what of Trais Johnson, was also a journey toward a greater understanding of what the *Bible* means in Ephesians 6:12, where it states, "For we do not wrestle against flesh and blood, but against principalities, against powers, against the rulers of the darkness of this age, against spiritual hosts of wickedness in the heavenly places."

Oakland thought to himself: *How could it be that after all these years and all the changes the world has undergone that this place, the very ground he was standing on was still being dragged down by immorality and hard living that surely everyone present had been warned against?* When Oakland thought about 6:12 in combination with what appeared to be a generational curse of some sort, something deep within him stoked his determination.

He wasn't sure about all he would find while re-visiting his community of origin, but he was certain that whatever he found would help him not only answer some of his own life's questions, it would also provide him some insight about the spirit of destruction that's been present here for as long as he could remember.

6

After a half-mile walk, Oakland's targeted destination came into view. As he neared closer and closer to the street where he and Tina grew up memories began stationing themselves before him like exhibits in a museum.

While walking down the block, still images of days gone by came to life bringing with them thoughts, smells, music, tastes, shared words. Whenever he lingered too long on any particular thing it was as if he had walked onto an active movie set; such happened after spotting a discarded lime green barrette, the plastic kind fashioned into a bow that snaps onto the plait of a girl's hair.

His friend, Beverly Gainesworth, would wear packages of them all at once in many colors. Her mama would press her wooly-cottony hair into many silkened pigtails that cascaded down her back and around her shoulders, and each one would be adorned with a different color barrette. He remembered she was fond of the red, yellow, and blue ones. However, he favored the lime green ones.

Oakland bent down and picked the barrette up out of the grass, like thunder a memory shot across his field of vision. Beverly's voice shouted like wind into his ears: "Help me!" In a rush, Oakland dropped the barrette, but it was too late. The memory was already reeled to play itself out.

It was a summer day, May 1988, Oakland saw Beverly running home, her barrettes a flurry of color and sound clacking against one another beating her shoulders. A group of kids were close behind, chasing her with hate and laughter.

"Say something else about how my daddy gone die," one of them shouted.

Beverly, up against a fence, cried, "I'm sorry. I, I'm just saying what I saw. I dreamt it."

One of the kids grabbed her by the collar, "Take it back, heifer! Take it back! My daddy ain't gone die."

Almost as if time stopped, she took her eyes off them and looked directly at Oakland. Though he was a couple years younger than Beverly, Oakland was taller, had muscles, and was known to fight.

"Help me, Oakland!" Beverly cried out, "Help me!" Oakland dropped his book bag, picked up the biggest stick he could find, and ran to her from across the street.

Oakland's long, strong, brown arms swung to and fro with ferocity. At the sight of Oakland rushing toward them and the sound of that stick slicing the air to shreds, the kids scattered.

Over the years, Oakland saved Beverly several more times.

The small group of people Beverly was able to help appreciated her gift, but those she couldn't help hated her. No one understood that she could not summon a vision or will herself to have one. She did not practice any form of sorcery or magic. She was just a girl gifted with sight into the beyond. Her gift was just as much a mystery to her as it was to others. Another thing that led to her falling out of favor with people was due to the fact that, as she got older, her premonitions became of the disciplining sort, which did not fare well with the impulsive crowd.

After a few of her warnings unfolded into tragic ends, she earned the name Bad News Beverly. That moniker and all that came with it led to her having a rather friend-less life.

Oakland remembered one time when Beverly attempted to re-connect with a young man she attended grammar school with. She shared a dream about him and revealed what evidently was secret behavior. What she said enraged him. One moment, she and the guy were peacefully talking about third grade; the next moment, he had a gun aimed between her eyes.

Fortunately for Beverly, Oakland was nearby again. He begged and pleaded on her behalf and just barely managed to talk the guy out of shooting Beverly right in the middle of her sixth sense. For this act of bravery, Oakland won Beverly's undying friendship.

After the near-death incident, regardless of how much time had passed, she always brought up how Oakland saved her life. Last time he saw her, in her late teens, she told everyone who would listen how he was her best friend and how he rescued her from being murdered. It didn't matter to Beverly that she had not seen or talked to Oakland in years or that it had been even more years since the incident.

Remembering Beverly's sweetness and childlike innocence, Oakland decided to keep the barrette. He held it for a moment, just to be sure he wouldn't be plagued with a deluge of thunderous memories. This time, all was quiet.

7

With the barrette in his bag, Oakland continued onward hoping for a familiar face that could answer questions about Trais Johnson. He knew better than to try and find Tina. He had heard years ago that Tina was in such bad shape, half the time she did not even know her own name. Based on all accounts, everything he'd heard about Tina having lost her mind was true. To that end, there was not one person of Trais's family he could contact.

He sorely wished he knew Beverly's whereabouts. Last he heard, she had gotten married and moved. And although he had done it before leaving home, he did yet another Google search, again—no results.

He thought, *Maybe I should just go looking for Beverly. She might be able to tell me something about Trais.* He imagined himself asking random neighborhood folk about her, then quickly figured that that might do more harm than good.

Exasperated, he looked at his map of the Austin neighborhood and tried to recall where people he remembered lived; however, he soon realized that the few friends he had that made it out were long gone from this place, and those he heard had remained were not the types he wanted to share such a sensitive matter with.

He felt more than certain that in the wrong hands his questions about a dead boy and Beverly would thwart his mission. Then, the thought of having to ask strangers about this young man's life *and* also having to answer their inevitable questions hit him hard. He felt ashamed. The shame of having to get information about a deceased young man who may or may not be his son embarrassed him; it gnawed at his sensibilities and made him feel like taking cover and hiding.

He did not want anyone thinking he was an absentee father who was doing too little too late, who had just recently had a flash of consciousness and sense of responsibility *after* a tragedy.

Oakland's fear of reproach made him think again about Beverly. Memories of the harshness many people of the community displayed toward her made him worry about being treated cruelly too. After a few deep breaths and several minutes of contemplation, he concluded he must push forward. He did not want to go to the police station without having more information and knew better than trying to get information from whatever school the young man attended. In his re-awakened despair, he closed his eyes and prayed for a miracle; upon opening them, he saw the numbers 124 on a torn lottery ticket that had a wad of bubble gum on the top and a slick of mud on the bottom. *124,* he thought. "124," he gasped as the numbers attached themselves to a memory; 5124 West Ohio was the building address of Beverly's extended family.

When Oakland arrived at 5124, the two-flat Greystone was nothing like he remembered: The window frames were worn, the lawn was unkempt, the curtains were mismatched, and the wood of the front porch was weathered.

It was very much unlike the dignified, courteous, aware of the power of presentation tradition that Beverly's aunt and uncle practiced. They always kept a tidy lawn with flowers that complemented their home's trim and their window dressings. They were incredibly neat people who greatly appreciated their property and showed it by dutifully tending to its upkeep.

But, this place with its broken this and busted that made Oakland hesitate approaching the door. Then, just before he thought himself out of the whole idea, he saw a charm that had been left in the yard; it was a silver G with small sparkling rhinestones bordering its edges.

Oakland figured chances were a Gainesworth still lived there. So he collected himself and powered forward hoping to get some help from an old friend.

When Oakland knocked on the door a feminine voice from inside told him to wait one minute. Oakland obliged. About five minutes later he heard the sound of locks disengaging, a door chain sliding and falling against the frame, and the creak of hinges. Peering into the small squares of the screen door, Oakland saw a young woman, no older than sixteen, a mass of hair, and a long dusty white gown.

Stale smells wafted from the house and assaulted his nostrils. The girl's long, sandy brown hair filled with knots and curls, moved stiffly as she looked at him from head to toe.

Oakland asked, "Is this the Gainesworth residence?"

"Yes," she muttered.

"Are your parents home?"

She explained to him that she did not have parents, she had a father, and that her mother was deceased.

"I'm sorry to hear that," Oakland said. "Please have your father come to the door." And with that, Oakland stepped back several paces and stood in the sun.

The next thing he heard was the door slamming shut. It hit the frame with such force that two ears of corn that were perched on the porch near a St. Jude sculpture rolled down onto the grass. Oakland waited a few minutes then headed back toward the door, just as he raised his fist to knock, it opened.

When the girl emerged from the shadow of the foyer, she had on a pair of jeans, a striped white and green T-shirt, yellow sneakers, and a green barrette unthoughtfully placed in her hair. In her hand was an obituary, she handed it to Oakland without saying a word.

Oakland took it and immediately saw the picture of his dear friend, Beverly. She had died two years ago to the date. He read the document carefully and paused when he reached the part that stated she left behind a daughter named Unice.

"Are you Beverly's daughter?"

"Yes, I am. My mother told me you were coming."

This time when Oakland stepped backward, he nearly fell off the porch. "Wait. What are you talking about?" he stammered.

"Just the other night, my mother told me a friend, her best friend would visit soon," Unice said with a smile full of awe looking not at Oakland, but at the miracle he was.

Oakland, with bucked eyes and a mouth he had to intentionally close, stared at Unice. Oh, how she looked like her mother, but wilder. Her complexion, smooth and deep and dark, the color of raisins. Her eyes, a golden-brown, fiery hazel.

Looking at her was like looking at her mother, but her frumpy untamedness was unidentifiable. So disheveled and bedraggled was she that had it not been for her physical features, no one could have made him believe that Unice was the daughter of his finicky and dapper friend.

The contrasts of everything got the best of Oakland. He needed verification, something to ground him. At once a flurry of questions shot from his lips. "So you live here with your father? Where is he? I thought this was your maternal people's property. I heard your mother married and moved away from here. What is going on? How old are you? What did your mother tell you about me?"

Unice silently listened to all of his inquiries. She said, "If you want all those questions answered, please have a seat."

She watched as Oakland slowly backed against the post of the porch's staircase and seated himself on the top step with his bag clutched tightly in his hands, all the while never taking his eyes off of her.

His fear of her was visible: the unblinking eyes, the careful movements, his feet positioned just so, in case he needed to run. As to not frighten him further, Unice placed her back against the railing facing him and sat down on the third step. There they sat, peering into each other's eyes, each bewildered out of their wits, yet trusting that the moment was fate.

"Well," she said, "I'm sixteen years old. I live here with my father. This property belongs to my mother's side of the family. You heard right, my mother did move and she did get married. She moved from the place she spent her childhood over at her grandfather's house over on Orpah, then many years later when she was around eighteen she moved to Tennessee. She met my dad there. This building here belonged to her great aunt, Pattie Mae. Auntie left mama this property when I was twelve. Against my father's wishes, we moved back here.

My father had a house and his own business down there, but mama had to come back to Chicago. Why? I don't know. She'd tell my dad, his name is Bar-Lee, 'Barlee, I got to go back. I don't know why I just feel it. It won't let me rest. I got to go back.' So, 'cause like always daddy love my mama, he left Kosciusko Small Engine Repair behind and moved here." Unice stopped, paused, allowed all of the feelings about the could have beens and the "maybe if we hadn't..." thoughts pass before continuing; she then picked up where she left off, "And now that mama's gone, he still can't leave. Daddy just won't let us leave. I don't know the why of that neither. However, I'm starting to get the feeling that everything may have something to do with you being here today."

Her last statement sent Oakland into a tailspin. He began putting together all of the memories and information he heard about Beverly since he'd moved to Carbondale. He thought about the last time he saw her. He recalled how she glowed and how pretty she was. He said, "Oh. She must have been pregnant with you when I saw her last; we were both down at EIU. Both of us had cousins graduating from Eastern that year. Yeah, that was about seventeen years ago, not long after my grandmother died. I was sixteen. Your mother would have been nineteen at the time."

Oakland's eyes brightened with tears, he placed his hands over his mouth. "Oh my goodness, Unice," he said. "After the graduation, when she was getting ready to leave, she placed my hand against her belly. She did it in this very roundabout way. I remember thinking, did she just put my hand on her stomach? But before I could confirm anything, she was whisked away for some pictures or something. I haven't seen or heard from her since."

Each paused, lost in the spin-off thoughts of their own and each other's memories. Just as Unice was about to ask Oakland his reason for being at their place, he interjected. Oakland sensed Unice's question and decided to give her some details that did not include Trais.

He said, "When I got here this morning to catch-up with some people I used to know, although everything here for the most part is as I remembered, all of it is still very different. Or maybe, I'm different. At any rate, everything feels so different than I thought it would. I did not realize how much people's opinions mattered to me." Oakland stopped for a moment to gather his wily thoughts. He looked at Unice. She did not even seem to be the least bit confused. So he continued, "Shortly after I got off the train my plans just started changing and I got on a completely different path. It was like I knew where I wasn't going, but I wasn't quite sure where I was going. I just knew, like your mother, I had to come back to the old neighborhood. I knew your great-grandfather's place on Orpah was abandoned. An acquaintance of mine told me that years ago, and that was the only place I could think of to reach your mom." Oakland paused then started again with downcast eyes, "I tell you what, I didn't know she had passed on."

Unice said, "It's okay." Then, motioned with her hands for him to keep talking. Although she dreamt of his arrival, she had not received information about why he was before her. His nearly constant fidgeting and looking around clued her into his search for something. She also noticed that when she mentioned her father, he looked regretful. He'd rub his palms on his knees and purse his lips.

The silence between them made Oakland feel the fear and embarrassment of his reason for being there, so he hurriedly continued, "Yeah. When I got here, I walked to the block where I grew up and was just looking around. My grandparents are deceased. My mom and brothers and sisters moved from here long ago. So without a connection, I started feeling lost. Then, like assistance from heaven, I looked down and saw the numbers 124 on a lottery ticket. That was all I needed to re-boot my vague remembrance of the couple times the bus driver dropped your mom off here. Unice, trust me, it was so long ago and so tucked away into the recesses of my memory that had I not seen that ticket I would not have ever even remembered this place existed."

Unice started to cry. A torrent of remembrances drenched her vision. All of the seemingly piddly coincidences that happened to her mother on what seemed like a daily basis that she once deemed minor were now being appraised under a different light. Just little small things that, looking back, made a big difference like found money, a remembered name, having just the right words at just the right time, an unusually helpful stranger, an opened door, a cracked window, a lock that had not engaged, a remembered friend. Unice sobbed as she recalled her mother's supernatural good fortune. The pain of the loss and the treasure of it all made her place her hands over her face and weep bitterly.

Oakland's eyes teared as he watched the mourning in her heart appear as beads of sweat along her hairline.

When Unice removed her hands from her face she said, "I always resisted my mother's gift. My mother was Southern Baptist. I'm like my father, I'm Catholic. Although I knew her gift was real, I hated it. Everybody thinks I look like my mama, and I do, but if you knew my aunt Mae Bell, you'd see I'm the spitting image of her. Mae Bell loved my mother with all her heart, but mama spooked Mae Bell, so Mae always kept her distance from her. I think I inherited that 'cause it really wasn't no reason for me to be as harsh as I was toward my mother. I detested all that singing and dancing and talking to God and speaking in tongues. I've always been very reserved, just like Mae, so Catholic traditions appealed to me. But, now, sitting with you today, I wish I had spent more time with my mama. I wish I had gone to worship with her more, learned more about her. Oakland, my mother was an amazing person, the best I've ever known. I let my pride and prejudice keep me from her, and ultimately it blocked her from blessing me."

Oakland looked intently at Unice and asked, "Blocked her from blessing you?"

Unice, while looking deep into the not too distant past, responded to Oakland, "About two years before mama died—by the way, none of us knew she was dying—it was two Christmases before her death, she started praying and fasting more than ever. Don't get me wrong, mama always prayed. She had a prayer life, like a real one, like for real. And she always fasted. She always told me, 'Give thanks to God. Thank Him for everything. Don't just say you grateful, show you grateful. Prove it.' I've always known her to fast and pray, since I was mama's little bitty. She said it brought her body and mind under dominion and into a place of pure appreciation. In those last couple of years, she really kicked it into overdrive. She even quit her job so she could serve the Lord full-time. We all thought she had gone crazy. Well, all of us except daddy."

Unice stopped before continuing. She smiled at Oakland's expectant eyes and how everything about his body language communicated he was interested in every word. She then said, "Well, anyway, the December before mama died, I remember the day, it was the last day of school, the start of winter break. I walked in the house; mama didn't hear me come in. She was in her bedroom screaming at the top of her lungs, 'Help her, Holy Ghost. Stay with her, Lord. Be with her, Heavenly Father in the name of Jesus. I pray that You be with her as You have been with me, Your faithful servant.' I ran over to mama screaming, stop it, mama, please stop. It was like she was in a trance. When she looked at me, and could finally focus, she said, 'Oh, my darling, my love, I was just praying for you.' When she said that, something about it made me so angry. I yelled at her, stop praying for me, mama. I don't like it. Leave me alone! After I said that, I saw her heart break. It was as if I could actually see it breaking. Then, for some reason mama reached for my head; she kept grabbing at it, and that's when I saw the oil on her hands. At that point, I became enraged. I would never hurt my mother, but that day I pushed her off me. I remember seeing her fall back against her bedroom door. After that I just left."

Oakland exhaled the air, he'd been holding in his chest then said, "Unice, I'm sure your mother forgives you. You were afraid and you were angry. When your mom and I were young, I cannot tell you how many people were confused and frightened to the point of violence when it came to her, so forgive yourself for that. I cannot believe, having known your mother, that she would hold that against you."

Unice with the countenance of defeat said, "Yeah, be that as it may. I still blocked my blessing. I don't have my mother's gift, not the way she had it. I can't help but wonder if she was trying to leave it with me, Oakland. I do believe for all the trouble it caused her, she still wanted to pass it on, like leaving a legacy."

Oakland, shocked by Unice's admission, said, "But you told me she told you I was coming."

Unice slowly and carefully explained the nuances. She said, "Yeah, but that's not how my mother's gift worked. Like me, she had dreams, but my mother's sight was complete when she was gifted a vision. She was kinda like Moses, but God spoke to mama in her dreams. Sleeping for her, when God had a message he wanted delivered, was like Moses going to Mount Sinai. It doesn't happen that way for me. I'll have a dream about my mother and learn things, and it only happens every once and a while, and it's all very sketchy and disorganized. But, mama, she was truly one of the Lord's set of earthly hands and feet."

Although Oakland felt for Unice, her admission about her own regret made him feel a bit more comfortable about the regrets he was carrying. After a few deep breaths and a long moment of silence, he finally said, "Speaking of hands and feet...." Oakland paused abruptly. The shame had returned. Just the words themselves being associated with him, just the thought of someone knowing that he did not know his son made him nauseous with humiliation. He quickly diverted, "Unice, do you know why I'm here today?"

She said, "No," then waited.

Oakland tried again to tell her, but the words would not come. In an instant, his grandmother's words came to him, "a closed mouth will not get fed." And although he could not tell her directly, he made himself say, "Unice, the reason I am here today is because I am in search of something I feel I may have missed in my life too, and I've decided to put my hands and feet to work to get to the bottom of it."

Oakland began explaining the happenings of the past several days, starting at the dentist office going all the way up to his arrival at the Gainesworth porch; however, his story was absent of the connection with Trais; in fact, Oakland did not refer to Trais much at all, he described him as someone who may be related to some people he used to know.

The vague reference did and did not happen on purpose. Each time he tried to be honest about the situation, he would become beside himself with his own pride. A pride that had actually sustained him in many positive ways throughout his life. Whenever he was faced with a task that made others turn back, Oakland would tell himself, *you're stronger, you're better,* and push through and get things done. It was this characteristic that made him an outstanding student, self-controlled, and a man who was not weak for all the things that men tend to stumble over.

However, that same pride was preventing him from being honest in the moment. Oakland could not accept such a significant level of failure in himself. All the men he had treated over the years, who had children here, there, and everywhere, he sincerely felt for them and all the things that caused them to be neglectful. But, he was also deep down inside repulsed by them. It was a repulsion made pure by his own abandonment forced on him by his very own absentminded, absentee father. And sometimes when Oakland became pressed in life and began thinking he may not have what it takes, he would fall back on and be strengthened by the thought that he did not become *one of them*. So, the anxiety possibly being one of them caused was real; thus, in the telling of his story, each time Trais was the motivating factor or objective, he found himself drawn to the distraction of concentrating on the inside of the Gainesworth house.

Unice could hear the disjointedness. She knew Oakland was leaving something, something important, out. She decided not to push the issue, and indulge his curiosities in hopes that giving on one end would allow her to take on another.

8

Each time Oakland got close to forcing himself to be more forthcoming, though the house was quite dark inside, it seemed to lighten in both energy and luminance. At one point it became so bright, Oakland switched topics altogether.

"So your mother lived here before she died, huh?" he said to Unice.

Unice noticed Oakland's eyes were firmly fixed on the foyer's floor-ceiling mirrors, which held the reflection of the living room.

"Yeah, she lived and died here. Mama died while sleeping in daddy's chair, the one you're looking at in the mirror."

Oakland quickly brought his attention back to Unice's face.

Unice continued, "She wasn't sick or anything. Her body just gave up the ghost. Would you like to go inside?"

"No, no," Oakland replied, "I'll wait until your father is home. I'm a grown man, Unice, and you are a child. You do not know me, and more importantly, your father does not know me. I have no business being inside your house alone with you. I'll wait for your dad to come home. If he invites me in, I'll go. So, thanks, but no thanks."

Unice was stunned silent by Oakland's response. Since as far back as she could remember, her father impressed upon her the importance of being observant. The day she turned thirteen, her dad brought her the *Unmasking Sexual Con Games* book. And before that he always made sure to let anyone Unice was involved with personally, academically, religiously, or otherwise know she had a father who cared and was watching over his daughter.

Unice would be deeply embarrassed as a pre-teen when her father would personally introduce himself to her peers and their parents. So well-associated was her father with her identity that everyone in the neighborhood, at school, and at church nicknamed her "BarLee's girl." It didn't help that BarLee Sprott looked like an African warrior, tall and muscular. Even his teeth looked strong, wide and white like perfectly shaped squares of bleached whale bone. And any-time Unice would complain to him about being her shadow, he'd say, "You are mine to protect and grow. Be patient. You'll thank me later."

Understanding came more quickly than Unice could imagine. She had heard rumors about sex, pregnancies, and abortions starting in eighth grade. By freshman year, Unice had seen several girls she was once friends with fall by the wayside. Girls she had gone to grammar school with could now be seen hanging out in alleys, drinking, smoking, getting pimped, and even recruiting other girls into prostitution.

BarLee was certain to share with Unice that she should have mercy and compassion on her peers and understand that their parents' lack of awareness contributed to their circumstances, and that she should be grateful for not only his love but his care too.

Unice was dumbfounded by what appeared to be a complete blind spot on their parents' part. It was if they didn't understand that children had to be taught how to think and act, how to respect themselves, and that they needed protection. It was as if their parents did not, could not, grasp the concept at all, nor how detrimental the outcome could be.

And the outcome was absolutely devastating. Unice would see her class-mates everywhere they were not supposed to be, and right in the middle of where they should not be. Unice's dad would be taking her to school and they'd be walking in the opposite direction; her dad would be taking her to church and they'd walk right by and not even stop to wonder; her dad would be taking her to gymnastics and they were not even interested.

The summer before her sophomore year brought more of the same bad news. By the time she was fifteen, even more of her classmates had gone woefully astray, and it was at that time she began to discern how certain types of people were capitalizing on their poor judgment. Often, they were the same ones who had seduced and groomed them into troublesome lifestyles to begin with.

She noticed men of all kinds, and some women too, leering lasciviously at children her age and even younger. However, it was abundantly clear that the freshly bloomed troubled teens were their favorite targets. Despite the fact there were many men and women who were upright, the non-right ones stood out, and craftily made themselves known at the most opportune and unfortunate time.

When Unice became a sophomore, it was clear to her that there were three kinds of adults in her community: those who ignored children altogether, those who fiercely protected the children, and those that preyed upon the children. Certainly, the most frightening of the three were the predators, whom she referred to as vultures.

It was common knowledge that one of the most dangerous features of the vultures was their ability to be anyone—a derelict; a coach; a teacher; clergy; a man; a woman; or another teen, who had already been indoctrinated into the lifestyle.

Unice witnessed first-hand on many occasions, from her privileged position of protected daughter, lives being destroyed by sexual deviance and immorality. However being both her father and her mother's child, she had a special, heightened sense and aversion to destructive behaviors. She had become a firm believer of the power and prevalence of the spirit of perversion and its ability to create reprobate minds.

So, Oakland's level of awareness and vigilance garnered him a respect reserved for those who resemble the air of honor her father consistently and authentically maintains.

Unice smiled, then said to Oakland, "You know, I only asked if you wanted to come inside because of the dream and because my father will be here shortly. He doesn't work on Mondays. He's only there now covering for someone who couldn't be there on time. He'll be here any minute."

Oakland said, "Any minute, huh. That's great. Yeah, I'll stick around."

Oakland pulled a bottle of water out of his bag and offered Unice one. She accepted, and they continued sitting on the porch in the approaching-afternoon sun.

"So, Unice," Oakland said between gulps, "Why are you home? Why aren't you in summer school?"

Unice responded, "I got sick the day after I had the dream about you. I dreamt of you Friday and was sick as a dog on Saturday. Until you got here, I had not stepped one foot out of the house. Daddy been nursing me back to health. The only reason he went to help out today is because I started feeling better last night."

Oakland took another look around their yard. It is as unkempt as Unice's hair. The state of her hair made a bit more sense to him now, she's been sick. But Oakland felt there was a bit of a mismatch between the caring man she just described and the state of the lawn and house. So puzzling it was altogether, Oakland decided to ask, "What kind of man is your father?"

Unice watched Oakland's eyes and the message they were conveying, so she tailored her answer to address his un-spoken query. She said rather nonchalantly, "He's a busy man, a single parent now. This place used to be in tiptop shape when mama was alive. They would garden together, do all the house-keeping together, we literally had the best-looking place on the block. But since mama's been gone, my dad just takes care of me. He doesn't worry with all of the surface-level upkeep anymore. I think if it was pretty here, like the way it was when mama was alive, it would remind him too much of my mom. I know I don't like doing all the things mama would do with us, even though I enjoyed them, it still hurts too much."

Oakland immediately felt bad for being so judgmental, and he felt terrible about being so self-centered that he did not even consider they were still grieving and were actively depressed. He was also a bit perturbed by Unice's insight-fulness. He could tell by the way this unusually perceptive sixteen-year-old had been holding her own in this conversation that she could have easily given an answer far richer than what his small thoughts had summoned; for this, Oakland took responsibility because he knew that had he only made the effort to convey that he cared about more than the condition of their yard, she certainly would have risen to the intellectual occasion.

He appraised his own thinking and asked himself, *Why am I so pre-occupied by something so trivial?* It occurred to him, yet again, that he was intentionally, though not fully aware of it, allowing his mind to focus its attention on other things, anything, to avoid dealing with the real matter at hand.

The situation reminded him of something his counselor once told him, "When you busy yourself constantly critically judging others, you never have time to confront or resolve your own issues." Oakland's eyes squinted and blinked at the wisdom of his words. To correct the matter and maintain their rapport, Oakland stated to Unice, "You impress me beyond words. It's obvious your mother and father have done well by you. What did they do differently than many others whose children fall by the wayside, as you say?"

Unice looked deeply into Oakland's eyes. The vibration of his voice had changed; it was higher, it alerted her instincts. She sensed that his question held more and that the question was something that was actually burdening him. She quietly questioned herself before answering. She thought, *He's a counselor he may just want my input to add to his cache of mental notes? But, no, something about this parenting thing seems deeper.*

Unice re-directed her attention to Oakland's face, the emotion in his eyes forced her to follow her instincts. She thought, *Yeah. This is a personal question. I hear him in my spirit. Something's up with him and this parenting thing.*

Unice cleared her throat before speaking. The underlying issue of the moment was starting to reveal itself.

"Well," she said, "my parents have not only loved me, they have deliber-atlely cared for me. When my mother was on this earth, she walked with me;

talked with me, had real convresations with me; she encouraged me to think, and openly praised me for listening. Her love, like God's word, is sown into my heart, the fibers of my being." She paused for a moment to give thanks for that special gift before continuing. "But Oakland," she said with thoughtful reflection, "I think the reason my spirituality, intuition, and wisdom are so advanced is because not only have my parents loved and cared for me, my father provided me and mama with a safe place to love, learn, and grow. All the terrible stuff you hear about men doing, my daddy don't stand for it from himself or anyone else. My father claims me. A righteous man loves, protects, and claims me. That alone sets me apart. Mentally, it frees me up to have higher thoughts and deeper understandings."

Before Oakland could respond, Unice said, "Speaking of angels. Here comes daddy now."

When Oakland laid eyes on him, he had to catch his breath. The man seemed to be visibly absorbing the energy of the sun. He was just a beautiful brother, a man's man. He possessed the look any young child would want of his or her dad. He looked able, strong, capable of doing anything. And he was all the more striking when his eyes met his daughter's. When Unice locked glances with her father, he made a show of picking up his pace. Oakland watched as they smiled from their souls and greeted one another with great love. It almost made him cry.

After entering the gate, BarLee said, "Who do we have here?"

Oakland stood up in the presence of this man and shook his hand with reverence. His first words were, "My name is Oakland McCall. Your wife was a dear friend of mine. May she rest in eternal peace."

BarLee's smiling lips tightened at the mention of Beverly. Unice instinctually grabbed hold of her father's hand.

BarLee's voice, at first bellowing, was now just above a whisper. "Thank you, brother," BarLee said. "Any friend of my wife's is a friend of mine. How can I help you today, Oakland?"

Oakland's lips hadn't moved before a gust of wind twirled around their beings. The plastic grocery sack Oakland brought with him collapsed onto itself, and through the thin tan plastic the green barrette could be seen.

When BarLee caught sight of it, his lungs inflated with air and his eyebrows nearly touched his hairline. Without moving his eyes, BarLee said to his daughter, "Unice, come in the house with me for a moment. Oakland we'll be right back with you."

Oakland stood stunned. He was not sure what was happening but agreed to stay put.

Unice and BarLee walked into their house and closed the door behind them.

9

After approximately five minutes, only BarLee returned. Oakland could see Unice in the foyer's mirror. She appeared to be cleaning. BarLee stood forearm-length away from Oakland. When he spoke his breath smelled of fennel and mint. "Oakland," BarLee said, "my daughter brought me up to speed on the details of your discussion with her. But, I find it strange she cannot tell me exactly why you're here."

Oakland, while standing in front of BarLee, another father whom would possibly understand, still could not get the words to form. He could not even push them beyond his throat. They lumped at the center of his chest between his will and his fear. They clumped, suspended, unformed, just thoughts without language. After an uncomfortable amount of time and BarLee staring at him face-to-face, Oakland willed himself to reach into his pocket and pull out the article. He handed it to BarLee.

BarLee read the headline, looked at Trais Johnson's face, then at Oakland's. He stumbled away from Oakland, held the article by the tips of his fingers and with his other hand supported himself on the porch. He did not need Oakland to tell him why he was at his doorstep anymore.

Oakland watched as the giant of a man go from looking like a warrior to that of someone who seemed to be descending into illness. "What's wrong?" Oakland stuttered. When Oakland looked into BarLee's eyes he saw a void that was not there before. Oakland watched the article fall from BarLee's hands and land on his feet. He stared intently as BarLee swallowed several times before answering his question.

BarLee had a few false starts before words actually came out of his mouth. His jaw seemed near paralyzed and his shoulders were severely slumped. When he finally spoke it was as if something had aged him a thousand years.

"Oakland," he said, "my wife married me because we are kindred spirits. The difference between her gift and mine is my beautiful wife's gift worked to warn people, to turn them back toward God. The gift I have been given is the ability to see into the darkness of people's lives who turned away from God. Although God has a hedge around me and is my protector, because my spiritual gift is so strenuous on my body, mind, and emotions, the Lord gives me the choice of when I can use it." BarLee stopped abruptly, looked Oakland in his eyes, then continued, "I will possess my gift as long as I live and love holy and do not adulterate my being." BarLee stared at the afternoon sun for a moment then said, "Unlike my wife, who was an open vessel, I am closed. My spiritual gifts are only open for predeterminations that are the result of unrebuked, unrepented generational transgressions."

Oakland shuffled his feet, unsure about what to say or how to say it. His fear at this point was inside his skin and rose up in the form of goose flesh. If he could have run and put the whole thing behind him he would have, but he had the distinct sense that running would be futile. Whatever was to unfold the action of the process had already begun. Suddenly, Oakland began feeling worsted. Blood rushed to his head, and his ears felt as if they had been stuffed with cotton. His neck felt stiff and his limbs heavy. Oakland was just on the verge of passing out when BarLee's voice cut through the energy that was overpowering him.

BarLee said, "Oakland, one night while my wife was sleeping, about nine months before she died, she began talking. She was not the type who spoke in her sleep, so I always paid attention whenever she said anything. That night, she said three times, 'The man with the green barrette. Help him.' The next morning, when I asked what she meant, she could not tell me anything. She had no recollection of any dreams and it did not make any sense to her. I would pray for answers concerning the statement, but nothing ever came of it. Well, not until now."

Oakland immediately looked at the barrette, then back at BarLee. He was going to tell him what happened when he found it and touched it earlier in the day, but he decided to let BarLee continue instead.

BarLee said, "The day the young man in the article died, last Thursday, I heard people talking about him while I was walking to visit a friend of mine. The closer I got to the intersection of Cicero and Lake the louder and more frantic the people became. I always walk pretty fast, so I was only hearing bits and pieces of conversations. I had heard a boy had been killed. Then, when I got to the bus stop, I saw pools of blood on the ground. As I stood there staring at that blood, Oakland, clear as day I saw the reflection of a green barrette, just like the one in your bag. I blinked, looked twice, closed my eyes, I all but got on the ground and touched where I saw it, but it wasn't really there.

That night, I had a dream about having to walk into a demon's lair to retrieve a book. Like the mission of Lot in Sodom, I had to venture into the depths of hell. See, people tend to think that all heavenly blessings and knowledge can be achieved by walking through the light; however, some must be fulfilled by walking through the darkness. I know you're here in search of what happened to that boy. I do not have any answers. All I know is you must be destined to pass through the gates of hell to get the answers you are in search of. I will not burden you with all the details of how I know this, but that woman you saw today."

Before BarLee could complete the sentence, Oakland blurted out, "Oh my! The one by the train with the boy. She had gray eyes. I looked at her and—"

"Yep, that's her," BarLee said. "Her name is Jaymel. She is possessed by the spirit of perversion. Within her is," BarLee quickly glanced down at the article then back up to Oakland's face, "access to Trais Johnson's story. We'll have to go through her to find out about him."

Oakland defiantly stood to his feet. "I will not," he shouted, "participate in anything like talking to the spirits on the other side. I can't have any parts of anything like that."

"Oakland," BarLee replied, "our Lord is the creator of all time and space. He sees into the hearts of men and can discern the just from the unjust. Everything we know and do not know, He created. I don't know why God gave me this gift. I do not know why God gave a donkey the ability to talk (Numbers 22:28). I do not know why He formed all that is in the earth, under the earth and in the firmament, or why He created sin, darkness, and devils and demons (Genesis 1:1; Colossians 1:16; John 1:3). I have no idea why any of these things are in existence. All I know is every now and again, He will send me on a mission to help someone attain revelation knowledge."

Oakland, feeling completely puzzled, slackened his face. He was not prepared for that answer nor was he in any position to argue against it without referring to another Biblical story that did not have yet another Biblical story to counter its claim. Although Oakland was well-versed in Bible knowledge and considered himself an apologist for the faith, he never imagined having to defend what was typically widely accepted amongst believers as demonic. This conversation and situation was a paradigm shift so dramatic that it left him stammering and stuttering at the level of thought. In fact, Oakland wondered, if he would he even buy into any of this thinking had he not known Beverly's gift and seen its abilities for himself. But, the problem of this crossroads was Oakland did know Beverly, and now, in this moment, he questioned if God made them friends because all of this was in His holy plan from the very start.

BarLee knew Oakland was deep in thought. From BarLee's experience, those who were selected for such revelations earned them through faith and works. Only people who God was walking-talking-real to allowed themselves the opportunity to exercise their faith in a way not bound by law. The God who never changes from age to age, has never ceased to produce miracles or be omnipotent, omniscient, and omnipresent. From BarLee's perspective, God was as miraculous as He's ever been, it was us who brought Him down into boxes and began dictating what He could and could not do. BarLee knew, although Oakland had not accepted it yet, that the reason why Oakland was here is because Oakland was ready to grow and have a more spiritually dynamic relationship with God.

Silence ensued long enough for Oakland to make it to the last phase of his decision making process. He figured he had come this far, he may as well go further. Before making the commitment aloud, he questioned his reasoning, *Lord, is this what it means to walk through the valley of the shadow of death? Does it mean we stand in the presence of the deceased? In the presence of things and people You have parted from this world?* These questions puzzled Oakland. He was torn within himself; just two hours ago, to even think such would have been sacrilege in his eyes. But what was he to do with the reality facing him? He could not reconcile turning away from finding out whether Trais Johnson was his son, and he could not live with the weight of always wondering what might have been if he turned his back on this opportunity. It was finalized. Oakland McCall would see this through. He placed his hand on BarLee's shoulder and said, "Brother, before we go can we please pray and sing a hymn together?" BarLee smiled at Oakland and said, "I wouldn't have it any other way."

Part Three
The Confrontation

10

After their lunch of kidney beans and rice, whole grain cornbread, and Unice's spiced iced tea, Oakland and BarLee prayed Psalm 23 with Unice and sang five hymns from the *African American Heritage Hymnal*. At exactly three o' clock, Oakland and BarLee left Unice at home after wrapping her in hugs and gratitude.

Oakland noticed that the neighborhood felt different walking alongside BarLee. Almost everyone who greeted BarLee asked about his daughter. He smiled each time from ear-to-ear and said, "My princess is doing better than ever." It made Oakland proud to see a father so overjoyed about having a daughter, and to see people enthusiastically responding to the connection that BarLee fostered with Unice.

The acknowledgment from the community was another layer of proof that the healthy father-child dyad is extraordinary in its ability to make a child not invisible.

All around Oakland, earlier that day, as he walked from the train stop to his destination, it was painful to watch the invisible children; those who were simply not seen and shrouded in neglect and purposelessness to the point of worthlessness.

Suddenly, Trais Johnson fell on Oakland's mind in the form of a shooting pain into his skull. He thought, *What if Trais Johnson was one of the invisibles?* Just the idea pained Oakland's heart so tangibly that he grabbed at his chest.

BarLee noticed the movement and asked Oakland if he was alright.

Oakland wanted to scream at the top of his lungs, I think Trais Johnson is my son! But he could not bring himself to do it. Witnessing how remarkable of a father BarLee is, Oakland felt small. He felt awful for being a grown man who did not even care to check back in with a woman he had slept with just in case something, someone had come of their union.

Oakland was embarrassed to think that someone of his own flesh and blood had been out fending for self in this big, dangerous world like a wild animal. Already, Oakland was deeply scarred by just the thought that Trais was possibly his son. And, if he was, he could feel the humiliation of Trais's death just waiting for the evidence needed to tidal wave over him and drown him into a depressive episode. Oakland knew in his soul that if Trais was his, he would never reconcile not having acted on all the feelings he'd had over the years.

Oakland realized that if he did not re-focus his attention elsewhere that the weight of his thoughts would bury not only his confidence but also his purpose. His childhood and the situation he was in at the very moment served as a reminder to him of the danger of what can happen when one allows dis-empowering thoughts to take hold, so in an instant, he decided to get out of his own head and turn his attention outward.

Another startling observation he acknowledged was that while walking alongside BarLee, the neighborhood he had been so critical of before appeared not as damned. Of course, all that he had observed earlier remained, but the good was certainly overpowering the bad now. For example, although there was much death and destruction all around him there was also abundant life and hope and people, all kinds of wonderful people.

And just as he had that thought, BarLee said to Oakland, "Hey, you see that guy standing next to the garbage cans over there?"

Oakland said, "The homeless guy? I mean, the homeless looking guy?"

BarLee said, "Yeah, him. His name is Mr. Jimmie Harris. Man, I'm telling you, you've never heard anyone sing Ave Maria the way he does, and in German too. It's beautiful! It brings me to tears every time."

Oakland took another look at Mr. Harris and was even more astonished that this guy with his inextricably tangled locs and clothing that was stained down to its inner fibers was capable of singing beautifully let alone in German. Without thinking about it twice, Oakland said, "Wow. He's bilingual. Okay. I'm sure he could find work if he cleaned himself up. If he's not severely mentally ill, or something."

BarLee continued looking straight ahead his eyes and smile fixed on his friend, he said to Oakland almost as an said, "You're right. But, Ol' Jimmie doesn't care about the things he used to. He was in the military years ago. He was an engineer. Things were going great for him. He had a beautiful fiancée from Sierra Leone, smart, a gorgeous sister. About two months before they were to be married, she had a miscarriage. They were in Germany at the time. She took it pretty hard. One day she told him she wanted to go back home and be with her family. He thought it would help her cope. 'Til this day, he never saw her again. It broke his heart. He said she was his everything and without her he didn't want nothing."

Oakland thought to himself: *I don't remember being so judgmental and negative? I could have easily surmised he was a veteran who fell on hard times. Why am I being so harsh?* Having been a professional problem solver for most of his adult life, he knew the best thing to do was hear the responses his thoughts retrieved, especially while in the company of someone as wise and conscientious as BarLee.

Oakland then said to him, "You know to look at Mr. Harris, no one would ever even guess that's his story. I immediately judged him as…well you know what I was thinking. I don't remember being this way. Wait! I know I wasn't this way. I was an underdog. I was him. People thought they knew all about me before knowing anything. Do you understand what I mean?"

BarLee with his voice slightly raised responded, "Yeah, I know. That's what happens when we read and watch from too far a distance. You are what you consume. And if you've been just consuming what Baraka refers to "as the lying rag," of course you're judgmental and only have a very few stereotypical default thoughts and categories to turn to. That's why we have to pull our heads out of these computers, newspapers and books, and stop relying on what someone who probably don't give two mites about the real story has written. Man, some of these writers and scientists base all of their information off of a quick look at some numbers and a half-baked understanding of some statistics and other manners of skewed biased measures. You have to know and talk to people for yourself. To someone on the outside, Mr. Harris just another Black bum and everything that implies. They'd never even think to guess the man may be as intelligent and talented as them, and his decision to be the way he is is based on how he's made sense of the world."

Everything BarLee said resonated with Oakland. He had not realized until this moment that everything he remembered about his childhood and this neighborhood was overwhelmingly negative. He thought to himself, *It's possible I never investigated the feelings and dreams I've had all these years about having a son because I despised coming back here. But why?* Just as Oakland thought "why?" the neighborhood began to change, it went from the poor working-class who had tattered screen doors and passable lawns to well-worn dirt, and houses that had more plywood for windows than glass. BarLee, looking straight ahead, pointed his finger, to the west and said, "Brother, that's where we're going."

Oakland looked in the direction of BarLee's finger and saw a dingy, white, wood frame house with peeling paint sitting on a lot with nothing but dirt and trash and old cars on both sides of it. In just eight blocks you saw the difference between people who were still hanging in there and those who had given up. Oakland felt that all that was wrong and was ever wrong in the nearby vicinity originated from the creepy abandoned looking house he was staring at.

Before they moved forward, BarLee warned Oakland that anything in his past, any secrets, any shames both hidden and forgotten would be used against him in his search for the truth.

At once, Oakland felt exposed and unsure. He asked BarLee, "What do you know about me?" BarLee assured him he knew nothing, only what he had shared. BarLee told him, "I'm a sort of guide. I can lead you here based on the knowledge the Holy Spirit gives me, but unless you say something about yourself, I won't know it. However, based on what typically happens, every demon in hell is going to try to stop you from grabbing hold of the blessing God has for you and that is done by throwing every iniquity, every immoral act, every transgression in your face."

Oakland paused for a moment. He stopped walking. He even stopped breathing momentarily. He was deathly afraid of uncovering his past. All the unanswered questions he had about himself, whole years he could not remember, things that people had said he'd done that he could not recall. The thought of it all being revealed to him made him shiver. But the feeling that he may possibly be a father pulled him forward and made him put one foot in front of the other.

Although Oakland was ashamed of BarLee finding out why he needed to know about Trais Johnson, he figured that if Trais was his son he deserved any torment God or anyone else could give him.

Oakland prayed within his own heart that if Trais was his son that God would accept this act as repentance for not having been there for him. A tear escaped Oakland's eye when he thought about Trais and how he died, how tortured his life must have been, or at least he hoped it had been considering what he'd done.

Expeditiously, Oakland reprimanded his own condemnatory thoughts and asked God to give him and Trais mercy. At once, a feeling came down around Oakland. It was one of concern and acceptance. His heart filled with love for the young man. The sort of fatherly love he hoped someone shared with Trais during his short life.

Suddenly, BarLee's words broke into Oakland's mental space with the power of a swift kick. It was then that Oakland realized he and BarLee were now standing directly in front of 5116 West Hadar.

BarLee said quietly yet sternly to Oakland, "You must be brave and stand against the sin and reproachable acts of your own heart and hands. When you step foot inside that house, Oakland, you're going to figure out real fast why God warns us against sin and an immoral thought life."

As Oakland slowly walked closer to the house, he noticed that BarLee stayed behind. "Aren't you coming?" he asked.

BarLee explained to Oakland that the spot where he was standing was as close as he was allowed. BarLee reminded Oakland of Deuteronomy, chapter 18, versus 10-11, which state, "There shall not be found among you any one that maketh his son or his daughter to pass through the fire, or that useth divination, or an observer of times, or an enchanter, or a witch. Or a charmer, or a consulter with familiar spirits, or a wizard, or a necromancer."

In an instant Oakland became incensed. "Why did you bring me here, BarLee?!" he yelled.

As calmly as he could, BarLee helped Oakland understand that the nature of the sin Trais Johnson struggled with in his life was the reason why he had to come to this place. "God will protect you, Oakland," BarLee reassured him. "But you must go alone. This is your journey. I will wait here for you. I will be praying for you while Jesus stands in the gap."

Oakland felt the blood drain from his face. His shoulders sloped downward. Fear excreted from his pores in the form of sweat. He envisioned what his feelings looked like and straight away recalled how BarLee's appearance changed after he had handed him the article. He felt himself growing exhausted, weak.

BarLee, shouted to him, "Stand firm. The Lord is with you."

Oakland placed his hand on his back pocket and felt for the paper he knew was there. He pictured Trais's face and resolved within himself to go on.

11

The street facing entrance of the home had a two-by-four covering it, so Oakland walked along the side of the house in search of another entrance. The house was unusually long. And, all along the drip edge of the roof, in the soffit, and on the fascia was black mold.

The once white paint, now moldy and greenish, laid in numerous piles of strewn flakes both large and small along the perimeter of the house. Two-by-fours and other pieces of wood were nailed diagonally across many of the windows. Some of the smaller windows were broken out and the wind created wild whistling sounds as it passed through them.

At the rear of the house, Oakland found a makeshift door. A large piece of plywood partially covered the passageway. Oakland could hear people inside. They were cussing and loud and making all manners of crude noises. He could smell alcohol and urine and hear the flicker of lighters. He shuddered at the idea of going inside.

From the direction of the alley, Oakland could hear someone approaching. A rundown garage blocked his view. However, from the sounds of it, a woman was drawing near. She was speaking loudly, rudely. She sounded like the kind of person who would be inside a place like this.

When she came into view, Oakland was surprised by how young she was. She looked to be about sixteen. She was a pretty girl, but she walked with the wide gait and showy posturing of the women who worked the track. Her shorts were too short and too tight for a girl her age.

It pained him to look at her. The little top she had on could barely contain her young body that was already tattooed, pierced, and scarred. It was clear what type of life she was accustomed to and it could be heard in the roughness of her voice.

"What you need?" she asked not looking at him, just seeing a man, another man.

Oakland quickly stepped to the side out of her way as she sashayed toward him never looking away from the entrance.

Her skin was the color of caramelized onions, taut and still smooth. Her hair was the color of russet potatoes. Her eyes—gray. She was the younger version of the woman he'd seen earlier with the young boy.

Alarmed by how much she looked like the woman, Oakland responded stuttering, "Ya, your mother."

That's when she stopped and whatever was jingling in her purse made one last clanging sound. "What do you want with my mother?" She asked. Then followed with, "Humph! If you really knew, you way too old for her!"

"Uhh, yes," Oakland replied, "Uhm, I have some questions for her."

That's when she looked Oakland in his eyes, looked over his entire face, looked down at his feet and back up to his hair. She sighed in a frustrated manner then said, "You're Trais's dad."

Oakland's heart sank. All the blood in his body rushed to his head. He couldn't catch his breath. Holding back tears, Oakland wheezed out, "Do you know what happened to my son?"

When Oakland asked the question, he saw something visibly come over the young woman. In that moment an indecent energy emanated from her being and made the hair on his neck stand. Although she had not physically moved one inch, whatever was in her was crowding him. The longer she stared at him, the closer it got.

Oakland shouted, "Greater is He that is in me" (1 John 4:4).

After Oakland spoke, the dark spirits that fight for her being made her turn on her heel and push the plywood that covered the door to the side. She opened it just enough for her body to shimmy through.

Oakland stood astonished.

After she disappeared into the darkness of the house, Oakland panicked. He could hear her speaking with people inside and them greeting her. "Hey, Queena," various people said.

Anxious and desperate, Oakland started yelling, "Queena, come back here! I need to talk to you!" The sound of people scrambling followed. Moments later, he heard a woman's voice; it sounded as if it was directly over his head, coming from the upper-level of the house.

"Who is that out there yelling your damn name, girl? Get him 'way from here."

Queena responded, "That's Trais's daddy, Mama."

"Trais's daddy?!"

Then Oakland heard another voice, a male voice. "Yeah, Jaymel. I peeked out there and that man is the spitting image of that boy. For real! Same everything."

That's when Oakland heard the Jaymel voice say, "Charlie, get him the hell on 'way from here. I ain't got a damn thing to say to nobody 'bout no damn Trais."

Her words infuriated Oakland. With his bare hands, he took the plywood and threw it to the opposite side of the yard. Inside, another door that led directly into the house had yet another piece of wood nailed across it, so that all who entered had to duck down before completely getting inside; Oakland kicked through that with the strength of a mule.

Straightaway, a pack of people ran past him and out the door.

Walking forward, Oakland yelled, "Queena! Jaymel! I want to know what happened to my son!" Come down here and talk to me now!"

The interior of the house, for the most part was dark and dirty and dusty, but in certain areas sunlight beamed in through window frames.

At his feet, Oakland saw all kinds of cans with burn marks, condoms, syringes, pipes, pieces of foil, blackened and bent spoons, and trash in various stages of disintegration.

In several corners of the room were mattresses. They were covered in stains and crusty clothing and pushed against walls that had obscenities written in lipstick, marker, pencil, ink and crayon.

The idea of Trais being in a place like this with these types of people filled Oakland with anguish.

Again, he yelled, "Queena! Jaymel!"

Coming from the front of the house, Oakland heard a noise. When he looked in that direction, he could see a man coming down the stairs.

As the man walked toward Oakland with his hands up, he said, "Listen, I don't want no trouble. I just want to get out of here."

Oakland looked at him. His body had been desecrated by drug use, and a large abscess was on his arm. Oakland assured him that he did not want any trouble either; he just wanted to know what happened to his son.

The man eagerly replied in a hushed tone, "Jaymel used to get down with your son, she upstairs," then he scurried out the door.

Oakland could hear Jaymel yelling at Queena. Suddenly, he heard a loud slap. As Oakland hurriedly climbed the stairs, he heard more slaps and curses. When he reached the top floor, there was a long, dark hallway; however, Oakland could see that at the hallway's end was a light-filled room. It was filthy much like all the rest, but inside it Queena stood holding her face and crying.

Oakland rushed into the large, murky, aqua colored room with its missing baseboards and junk everywhere. He marched up to Jaymel and yelled directly into her face, "Do not hit her even one more time!"

Jaymel and Oakland stared each other down. Then without missing a beat, Oakland said, "And, tell me what you know about my son! I know you knew him!"

Jaymel laughed at him viciously.

Her callousness filled him with resentment and terror. Again, he exploded, demanding information about Trais.

Again, the same reaction from Jaymel. The darkness that manifested from her being was strong, and it made Oakland's body involuntarily quiver.

Oakland stepped back to get a good look at her.

As she laughed the contortions of her face revealed different features. He noticed she appeared to be in her late thirties, but could look either older than her age or younger. It was eerie and disconcerting watching her morph and recast from old to young and back again.

He stepped into his fear and lunged toward her, grabbed her by the shoulders to make her and all within her still, to bring this transmuting body of hers under control.

However, when he took hold of her, his mind was seized. The evil forces within her dominated Oakland memory and possessed his senses.

It was immediate: The moment his fingers sank into the flesh of her shoulders, his mind was hers, not his own. At once, mentally, he was dragged to a dark place.

Oakland could see Jaymel, as a child, being raped by a man whose face she could not see. Her little legs with dainty socks folded down neatly at the ankles were opened wide on top of a washing machine as the bad man moved between them.

The sadness, the hurt, the confusion she experienced in that moment, felt like hot dope coursing through Oakland's veins, and it took dominion of all it came in contact with. Oakland's saliva foamed in his mouth, and bubbled at the corners of his now slack lips.

Oakland wanted to get away from Jaymel, but he felt weak, and she had wrapped her arms so tightly around him that he could not free himself.

Jaymel, with the strength of three men, pulled Oakland tightly to her, and in a voice unlike anything Oakland had ever heard, she said, "You want to know! Now know!"

In less than a second, her power over him intensified, and Oakland became the fourteen-year-old Jaymel.

He could feel the ominous energy of the pitch black room her young body had lain in. Alcohol permeated her being. The sounds of many men's voices filled the atmosphere. One by one, they climbed atop her, forcing themselves inside, biting her breasts, pushing her deeper and deeper into the unknown mattress.

Without warning, everything stopped and became even darker than it already was. Oakland began living the blackout Jaymel suffered, which was brought on by the force of the men and the alcohol they filled her with.

Oakland wept. His mind was exhausted, and his body had been ravaged. The little strength he still had in his soul came forth; he was in his rightful realm again. He pleaded for her to let him go. He tried but failed to squirm out of her grip.

The voice bellowed, "No, I'm not letting you go yet, you still want to live."

The words echoed in Oakland's ears and made his pulse quicken. The beating of his own heart could be heard loudly throughout the room. Oakland's fear provided him with a bit of adrenalin, but it was no match for Jaymel's arms. His resistance made her squeeze her arms around him tighter. Tighter. And tighter still. Again, he was immersed in a memory he recognized.

Oakland could see himself. He was small, just a young boy. His hair was cropped low, his little Fat Albert and the Cosby Kids shirt fit tight against his frame. The sun shone through red monkey bars as he played in the lot of his elementary school.

It was early on a Saturday morning. His mother rarely paid much attention to him, so he was able to slip away to his nearby favorite fun area. Being six years old with the playground all to himself was exciting. Oakland swung, and climbed, and jumped and skipped with great enjoyment.

Not long after he arrived, he noticed a rather tall figure quickly approaching, coming from the direction of the sand pit. Before he could do anything, a hand was over his mouth and he was off his feet.

Oakland kicked the body that was holding him, and screamed into the gasoline smelling hands that muffled his cries and smashed his nose. Before letting him go, the person fondled and squeezed between his legs.

As quickly as it happened, it ended. He was in the air one minute and pushed to the ground the next; however, the subconscious mental and spiritual aches and pains and influences never ended.

Until this very moment, the suppression of that memory was airtight. In Jaymel's arms, Oakland whimpered helplessly. He pleaded with Jaymel to stop and let him go. His petitions were mere whispers, breathless and inaudible. His neck was flimsy, and his head bobbled against her shoulder.

Queena watched in horror as Oakland became weaker by the minute. She had long seen her mother wield her looks and power over men and boys, and seduce them into being zombie like creatures, but she had never seen anything like this. It was otherworldly and formidable.

All Queena ever knew of herself and her mother was their lifestyle of men, fast money, and drugs. She knew her mother had a strange sort of pull in the streets and could get certain types of men and boys to do things others couldn't.

Colorism was a major problem in their community. Although there were prettier, nicer, and far more virtuous women for people to choose from, it was the combination of Jaymel's gray eyes, voluptuous body, and silky light brown hair that seemed to mesmerize most people, especially the pimps, gangbangers, and drug pushers.

Queena could hardly remember anything other than the conniving, game playing, hustler her mother had become. She had foggy memories from early childhood of her mother being a decent person, before all of the drugs and the rapes.

Sometimes, Queena would look at her mom and still see the little girl inside. That little girl was always hurt, but she was also innocent, sensitive, and very sweet.

Queena could not forget, though she tried many times, the first time she came face-to-face with the worst part of her mother. It was a few months after Queena's father, Tom, stopped coming around. He just up and disappeared one day.

Jaymel waited and waited and asked and asked. She even pulled Queena along as she went looking through other folks' windows and knocking on doors.

After two months of searching and not finding, one night Jaymel stood in the middle of the street yelling Tom's name. Even when the cops came, she did not stop. There wasn't silence until a couple EMTs came and shot something in her arm and took her away.

That's when she took to staring out the window most of the day, and hanging in the streets most of the night, and that's also when the men started showing up in droves.

They brought with them funny smelling smoke, and lighters, and pipes, and the white misshapen little pieces of stuff that they would put in the pipes until it sizzled and cracked. Queena, even with her young eyes, noticed that when all of that moved in, everything of any value moved out, including whatever good was left in her mother.

Jaymel continued squeezing Oakland, suddenly he cried out, "Please, Uncle Dakari, don't make me do it." This statement immediately resonated with Queena. Those were her words. At the speed of thought, Queena began putting two and two together; the tears on Oakland's face now were her tears, somehow Jaymel was making Oakland live the pain in her life too. Queena looked on dumbfounded as she remembered the day of the night she said those very words.

Queena could not have been no more than nine when it happened. Her mother asked her to dance in her bikini for Dakari and some of his friends.

Standing in her panties and bra, Jaymel told Queena, "Honey, just imagine you're at the beach. Put on the pretty yellow bikini Uncle Dakari bought you. We're just gonna dance a little bit, like they do on TV."

At that moment, the music turned up, and some of the guys started throwing money on the floor. Jaymel looked at the tens and twenties and ones and fives. Without even a hint of the kind voice she had just moments earlier she swatted Queena on her rear, pushed her toward the bathroom, and said, "Hurry up. Get changed."

Very few things made Queena cry, but this memory, this one brought bitter tears that burned every time.

Queena hated the men as they closed in on her with their hot breath and their clammy hands, but what hurt her worse was the way her mother with wide, wild excited eyes looked at them as they assaulted her.

Queena never forgot those eyes—how they appeared more opaque than usual—how they pulled the energy from her, and tugged at her very soul. She also never forgot how later that night, her Uncle Dakari pulled at her too and her swimsuit, and laid each on the floor.

Breaking from the memory, Queena looked at her mother in this moment and saw that same wild look in her eyes as she held Oakland captive in her arms. Queena looked at Oakland and saw the way she felt when her uncle touched her naked body as her mother continued dancing in the next room.

Queena, while looking at Oakland, did something unusual; she prayed to God, "Lord, don't let this happen."

It wasn't a moment later that Queena heard the familiar voice of a classmate. She could not identify the voice by name, but she remembered it from school. "Queena, Queena," it called from the back yard.

Queena composed herself and walked over to the glassless window frame and said, "Unice, is that you?"

"Yeah, girl."

"What are you doing here?" Queena asked.

Unice yelled, "Is there a man up there who came looking for his son?"

"Yeah. But how did you—"

Unice did not wait to listen to what else she had to say. She immediately began doing as she had been instructed in her dream.

Unice followed Oakland's path. She walked through the dark house, but while doing so she called on the name of the Lord and prayed the Twenty-third Psalm.

As she climbed the same stairs Oakland had climbed, with every step she prayed louder and louder.

Crowded in the hall leading to the room where Oakland, Jaymel, and Queena stood, Unice could see the demons of hell. She had to walk through them to complete her mission.

The perverse spirits intruded her peripheral vision and committed awful sins against children, women, and men. The smell of their beings were like bacterial infections, and the noises they made were a mix of mourning and fake satisfaction.

Unice's stomach turned and her eyes watered. She screamed, "'Though He slay me, yet will I trust in Him.' Blessed be the name of the Lord" (Job 13:15).

In an instant, the demons retreated. Then, they reappeared. They were beautiful, stylish, smart, and interested in her, only her. They surrounded her with feelings of warmth and adoration. So, she prayed louder and kept pushing forward, still making her way to the room, getting closer and closer.

That's when the demonic spirits jumped at Unice and attempted to distract her with salacious sexual acts, but they were no match for the Godly upbringing and inspired Word her Heavenly and earthly father had imparted to her.

Unice had been trained better: She could not be seduced by sex and its trappings. As her will triumphed over Satan's attempts, Unice victoriously yelled, "Praise the Lord," and entered the room.

With her spiritual eyes, she could see the power in Jaymel's arms had caused Oakland to fall from atop the rock of his faith. Unice prayed as she watched his soul lying on the threshing floor.

Unice placed her hands on Jaymel. Jaymel laughed. Unice prayed. Jaymel cackled.

Unice, looked over at Queena and said, "Are you a believer?" Queena, without hesitating, professed her faith. So, they joined hands and prayed for the Lord to give them Holy Ghost power. After their prayer, Unice told Queena to bless the room with the oil she had in her bag, and make the sign of the cross on every surface, and to never stop praying.

As Queena prayed and marked every surface of the room with oil, Unice turned her attention back to Oakland. Jaymel was face-to-face with him. Her arms were hugged around him. His arms dangled at his sides.

Unice stood with her chest to Oakland's back and wrapped each of her oiled hands around his wrists.

Jaymel continued squeezing him and yelled obscenities into Unice's face.

Unice very calmly said to Jaymel, "get ye behind me, Satan."

Oakland, sandwiched between Unice and Jaymel, grimaced from the pressure. He did not know what was happening but he felt the warmth of Unice's skin and the pressure of her being.

Unice began praying fervently. The more she prayed, the more cognizant Oakland became of his strength being restored.

The memories of his own abuse that he had forgotten, and the memories of abuse Jaymel and Queena had experienced—all of which he had been exposed to—the misery of it, the grip it had on him, the weakness it put in him, all of it began to fade and lessen in intensity.

All the darkness that had infiltrated his mind and that had been released into his spirit began being overcome by a marvelous light. The light was small and dim at first, but as the oil absorbed into his skin it began to sparkle and shine; its colors twinkled and glowed and cascaded in rays all through his mind.

Just thirty minutes earlier, while sleeping in her father's chair, Unice saw the same light Oakland was seeing. Unice dreamt of her mother on many occasions, but today, just minutes prior to this event, in her dream her mother touched her.

Just as Beverly had wanted to when alive, she made the sign of the cross upon Unice's forehead and passed on to her only child the gift of sight that the Lord had given her.

After her mother touched her, Unice immediately had a vision. She saw Oakland in a room fighting for his life; she saw Queena too, in the same room with Oakland but rendered helpless by fear and doubt. She said aloud to herself and heaven, "Lord, I will go." In an instant, she was given all that she needed.

With Unice's hands on Oakland, even Queena could see that strength was returning to him. As he became stronger, the muscles in Jaymel's arms which were once tight and defined and unmoving began shaking. Queena began praying harder and louder and rejoicing over God's power.

Unice whispered into Oakland's ear the vision she been given. As she spoke, Oakland, behind closed eyes could see colors flash, images coming to him in sparks.

Unice said to him, "You had a son."

Oakland with a voice that was being revived every moment said, "Yes, Trais Johnson is my son."

Unice responded, "His mother only told her closest family members. She was a terribly broken young woman who never rested in Christ. She was very strong-willed and never surrendered. Trais was an exact mixture of the most broken parts of you and his mother—his insecurities, his lack of awareness, his anger, his self-loathing, his severe loneliness."

Jaymel gripped her arms around Oakland tighter and cursed and yelled as Unice spoke.

Unice said to Oakland, "Do not be deterred. Keep your focus on the light and me. Stay with me. Remember your purpose. What did you come here for?"

Oakland feeling stronger though still very weak said, "I want to know what happened to my son."

Unice explained to Oakland, he would have to go through Jaymel because she was the one who had passed on to Trais the spirit of perversion. It was through Jaymel that seven other unclean spirits gained access to Trais, and eventually led him to the actions that led him away from God and to his death (Matthew 12:43-45).

Unice said, "Oakland, you'll need to have great courage and even greater faith."

Oakland immediately said, "I will do what I must."

Jaymel continued cussing and threatening them both while holding on to Oakland with all her might.

Unice, undeterred, shouted out next steps to Queena and Oakland.

Then, as a chorus, Unice, Oakland and Queena began saying, "We are reconciled to God. The love of Christ compels us" (2 Corinthians 5:14). Over and over again, they said that until Jaymel's arms fell to her side and under holy dominion.

Unice screamed, "Queena, get behind your mother make sure she stays standing. And, Oakland, hurry place your hands on Jaymel's shoulders!"

Queena did as she was told, and Oakland, fully restored, did as instructed.

Unice said to Oakland, "Keep your mind on God being the author and finisher of our faith; He knit us together in our mothers' wombs. The Scripture states in Psalm 139, 'Thou compassest my path and my lying down, and art acquainted with all my ways.' Oakland, make your petition to God! He is omniscient; if you accept this about our Heavenly Father, you will position yourself to receive divine knowledge."

At that moment, Oakland said, "I believe." Then, he gripped both of Jaymel's shoulders in his hands, and said, "Lord, I don't care how dark the valley is, please show me, give me the lessons of my son's life, and please forgive me, Heavenly Father, and his mother too. I repent of my sins, Lord."

It was like fire! Oakland's whole being burned with revelations. He saw it all. All the people over the years who had looked at, thought of, and touched him, Tina, and his son inappropriately. He also saw the wickedness of his own heart, the hidden lusts and the obscene thoughts.

Oakland wept as his confession began pouring out of him and broke the stronghold fear had on his subconscious.

In that moment, Oakland spoke the most shameful secret of his heart as if he was in a trance. With his hands still on Jaymel's shoulders, he spluttered, "Since I left here all those years ago, something never stopped stirring inside of me. I would have dreams, talk in my sleep, and have to quiet the voices in my head. I knew in my heart, I had a son. I just did not want to believe it. I was afraid. All the times I had been molested and all the awful habits, thoughts, and feelings it left me with, all the fear, all the demons it had injected into my life, I was afraid that whatever was in those people who had touched me had gotten inside me. I never wanted to unleash that on my child, so I stayed away. Now, he's dead. Instead of trusting God and being a father to my son, I treated him like he didn't exist. Instead of claiming him, I rejected him, and the devil took him. I could have saved him. I could have protected him." Then, Oakland yelled out a cry that shook the fixtures.

The pain of Oakland's life permeated all that was living. The mice that had been scurrying stopped in their tracks, an alley cat mewled in grief, a passing dog howled long and hard.

Unice and Queena, though sobbing loudly, continued to stand in faith with Oakland, and prayed for him to soldier through the pain and focus his energy on God.

It took a minute before Oakland could pull himself together enough to re-focus his attention. He then softly began asking for God to intervene, to provide answers, to bring peace.

Suddenly, all that was around them was calm and quiet. Even the bit of mumbling that Jaymel was doing stopped.

Unice sensed the moment was upon them. "Oakland, listen to me," she said, "Keep your eyes closed and your heart and mind open. Place your hand over Jaymel's heart and ask God to give you access to your son."

With his hand pressed hard against Jaymel's chest, Oakland breathed in deeply, prayed silently, and brought all of his energy into the space between his palm and Jaymel's beating heart. With his eyes closed, he listened and watched closely for a miracle.

Not two minutes passed before he heard something.

"Unice," Oakland shouted, "I see everything, generations, whole lives, centuries, space, galaxies. There is no time here. I see all of life, all through time!"

Unice responded, "Yes, Oakland. Like there's a landscape in this realm, in the heavenly realm there is the spiritscape. Remember, we serve a God Who is "spirit," Who is timeless. The *Bible* states, 'Beloved, do not forget this one thing, that with the Lord one day is a thousand years, and a thousand years as one day'. So, yes, Oakland with God there is no time. God is not bound by the laws of time" (2 Peter 3:8).

Silence ensued as Oakland continued looking into the great beyond, the spiritscape. He concentrated with all of his might and kept praising the Most High; then said, "I see two people one is much taller than the other. One is a child. They are way far off in the distance."

A few more moments passed before Oakland went on, he said, "There are two boys. One is a small child, a toddler. The other, oh Dear God, that's my son. That's Trais."

Oakland paused again. His eyes squinted stiffly while still closed. With great sadness in his voice, he said, "Torment and illness and pain is all around Trais. But, the younger boy," Oakland choked on his words, "I sense he is the little boy my son...molested. He lives. He walks in the light of the Lord."

What was confirmed next almost made Oakland fall to his knees.

Oakland muttered, "He prayed for my son, Unice. That dear boy prayed for my son, even after what Trais did to him."

Although Oakland was joyful about the prayer and the vision, he hurt sorely for Trais and the boy.

Oakland asked again, he whispered, "God, please tell me about my son. What happened to him? How did he spend his final days?"

Without warning, a feeling of urgency overtook Oakland. The image of the little boy Trais molested dissipated, and only Trais was left standing.

In the earthly realm, Jaymel's body began attitudinizing lasciviously under Oakland's hand. She also laughed loudly, and screamed, "I did to him what was done to me!"

Oakland nearly pulled away from the evil of it all, but he could not. His faith would not let him. So, he pressed his palm harder against her chest and yelled, "What happened to my son?"

Suddenly, the spiritscape trembled. And Trais started running in Oakland's direction, all the evil, all the good, his entire life ran at Oakland.

Oakland hollered, "He is coming toward me, Unice! My dead son is running toward me. I don't want this. Make it stop!"

"Do not be afraid. Stand firm. Call on the name of the Lord," Unice commanded.

Oakland shrieked, "He's getting closer! Jesus, help me. His energy is too much. He is getting too close! I can't take it!"

Unice yelled, "Do not be afraid, Oakland! The Lord has placed a hedge around you. Do not cower, let Trais run forth! Believe in the protection of your Heavenly Father."

Unice's words affected and effected Oakland. He roared, and pressed his hand against Jaymel's chest even harder. "Blessed be the name of God forever and ever, wisdom and might are His!" Oakland screamed.

Oakland pushed harder and harder, and harder still against Jaymel's chest. Trais ran toward him faster and faster.

As Oakland bawled and screamed, and continued pressing his hand against her chest, at once he saw just his hand in the spiritscape. In that realm, his hand glistened with power, so great and so mighty was it that it pushed through the hedge, and his son's whole being ran directly into the center of it.

Everything about Trais absorbed into Oakland's hand and fractured into glowing vibrant sparkling rays of gentle yellows and pinks, greens and blues and white.

In the colors were all the sights and sounds and voices of all the people his son had contact with during the last days of his life.

Quicker than the twinkle of an eye, Oakland was back in the earthly realm. He opened his eyes and saw Jaymel had fallen from Queena's arms; she laid sprawled on the floor, her legs folded underneath her body.

Unice grabbed Oakland's shoulders and turned him around to face her. "We are not done yet," she said. "There's more."

With tremendous gentleness, Unice grabbed both Oakland's hands, and both re-entered the spiritscape.

Unice asked, "Oakland, can you see what I see?"

"If what you see is a road."

"Yes, Oakland. I see a road. Do you recognize this energy surrounding us?" Unice asked.

Oakland said, "That is the energy of the angel. The angel the Lord sent to help me cross over. It was my strength as I broke through to the other side of the hedge where my son's spirit was."

Unice smiled. "Yep, Oakland, that's it," she said.

At once, an angelic energy took Oakland's hand, the hand that had pushed through the hedge. In an instant, all of the sound and visions and knowledge and light and darkness that was absorbed earlier by the hand, flowed from it and became pages and pages of thoughts and the details of lives.

The pages flurried around them, covered the road, and shuffled around their ankles. Suddenly, the sky opened and another angelic energy began gathering the pages one by one.

Then, there were three, three beings of great and wondrous light. Oakland and Unice looked at them in awe and with great reverence. In the angels' grasp, the pages became bound into a neat and orderly book.

The book was placed into Oakland's hand. Afterward, a great wind ascended the spiritscape into the invisible and descended Oakland and Unice back into the earthly realm.

When Queena could tell that more than just their bodies were with her, she immediately ran over and hugged Oakland and Unice. As they embraced, each of them thanked God for all He had done.

Had Queena not personally experienced the miracle that had occurred before her eyes, she would have not been able to fathom the possibility of the omniscient knowledge that sparkled from the pages of the book that Oakland was now holding.

"What is that?" She asked.

Oakland with visible joy heart said, "It is a story about my son's life."

Queena, for the first time in her life, said aloud, "Heavenly Father, Your mercy and power are worthy of praise," then in the same breath said, "Y'all have to go," and hurriedly began collecting Unice's belongings.

Unice stopped Queena from moving, looked at her earnestly, and told her, "If you're done with this life. My daddy and I will help you."

Queena burst out crying, "Unice, while y'all were doing what y'all were doing, I was telling God I cannot stay here anymore."

Without delay, the three walked through the house to its exit. As they left the property, they could hear the beams and the floorboards groaning.

When they got outside, BarLee was still standing at the front of the house. He smiled big and bright when he saw his daughter's face. "How? What? How'd you get here?"

Unice, with an excitement she could not contain, said, "Daddy, I fell asleep not too long after you and Oakland left. I had a dream, Daddy. Mama touched me. I received a vision and came here to help Oakland and Queena. I took the alleys and went in through the back. You were here out front all along?"

BarLee laughed and said, "Yes, I've been right here."

Oakland marveled at BarLee, "I cannot believe you're still here."

BarLee said to Oakland, "From the time we got here 'til now, it's only been an hour."

Neither Oakland, Unice, nor Queena could believe that, but after checking their cell phones, it was true.

On the walk to 5124, Oakland and Unice and Queena talked over one another. Their excitement was jubilant and out of control. BarLee could tell that Queena would never be the same, and explained to her that as long as she walked in the light, she would have a home with them and could consider him her earthly father.

When BarLee said that to Queena, Oakland stopped walking and stood still. His smile and enthusiasm withered. He pulled BarLee aside and told him, "I couldn't tell you this earlier, but Trais Johnson is my son. He's the reason I'm here. I was just...just too ashamed to tell you, anyone for that matter. But, especially you, you're an exemplary father, and I didn't even listen to my own heart and come see about my son. I'm humiliated by my actions, and I feel worse when looking at you and seeing what I could have been."

BarLee said to Oakland, "Brother, look at it this way, at least you have the decency to be ashamed, a lot of people don't. Being ashamed of the wrongs you've committed is a blessing, it's a sign of growth."

Oakland agreed with BarLee then said, "But, had I been brave enough to investigate what was bothering me all these years, I could have prevented all of this. My son could have had his dad."

BarLee pointed at the book in Oakland's hand and said, "This right here, what you've done today, you did that because of the great love you have in your heart for your boy. It's not like he's alive. It's not like you have anything to gain. You're here, you went through all that because you love him. Have no fear, Oakland, God will make it right. God would not have done all He's done and blessed you like He has if He wasn't going to right this somehow."

Although Oakland knew he had been forgiven by God, he was still very much in fear of being rejected by BarLee, this man he had only known for a few hours, who felt like a father, a close brother, even a minister to him.

BarLee's kindness and understanding lifted Oakland up; his words made him feel better about himself, and made him more clearly see the purpose of the struggle they had all just endured.

When they got back to Unice and BarLee's place, five hours of daylight were left. Oakland asked when they entered the yard, "Do you all want to hear my son's story?"

Unice, BarLee, and Queena looked at one another, then at Oakland. Unplanned and in unison they each said, "Uhh, yeah."

Rapidly, they prepared for the reading. Unice and Queena made refreshments. Oakland went to the corner store for popcorn. BarLee swept the front porch, cleaned the yard, and brought from within the house the most comfortable chairs he could find.

Twenty-five minutes later, they were all seated and ready. They said a prayer, then Oakland opened the book.

12

He read:

Hundreds of miles south of Chicago is Little Egypt, southern Illinois. It is a capacious region that is both southern and northern in its offerings. Ethnicities from all over the world gather here, drawn by its down home hospitality, its small-town conveniences, its intellectual capital, and expansive, untouched green lands.

The convenience stores have fresh fruit, newly picked from southern Illinois' trees. The people still farm, raise horses, cows, chickens, and goats. They grow corn, shell peas, and pick okra. The houses still have space between them.

Lush grass is everywhere. Wild flowers bob, cats sit on windowsills, and dogs watch birds synchronize their wings and fly.

People smile when they drive by. They wave to each other in the morning; ask, "how was your day?" when they come home in the evening, and remember each other during the hours in between.

§

When the sun rises up high and unblemished on summer mornings, it hits the Redding's house first; it invites itself right in, shines through the kitchen, beams over the floors, and meets its match on Eddie Redding's anointed face.

"G'mornin' baby," Lahteese Redding, Eddie's mama, says. "How's my sugar? Is he feeling as sweet as he looks?"

Eddie smiles a snaggle-toothed grin and says, "Yes, ma'am! Can I go play?"

Lahteese looks at her six-year-old, her first and only baby, and her womb stirs. He's so precious—son of the only man she's ever loved (besides her daddy, of course). She goes and stretches her palm over the smoothness of his face, feels the wool of his hair, kisses him on each eyelid, and holds him tight.

She tells him, "Of course, my precious. After you get cleaned up and have breakfast. Mama made you some biscuits, sweet milk, and that oatmeal you like."

Baby Eddie kisses and hugs his mother, does that dance that only six-year-olds know how to do, and rushes to the bathroom—little blue shorts, little blue shirt, pitter patter, pitter patter, gurgle, gurgle, gurgle.

§

"Stop eating those biscuits so fast, son," Lahteese says.

Eddie's mind is already outside, outside on their three acres of land, playing in the grass, swinging from the trees, and skipping down to the patch of jonquils that are in the center of the field. He finishes his breakfast quickly, attempts to clean his plate and bowl, then takes off running down the hill for that patch.

Looking after him, you see nothing but a trail of red dust, and hear everything that is the sweetness of honey child giggles playing patty-cake in the pleasant atmosphere he always leaves behind.

Lahteese hollers, "Be sure to get back here boy, before your daddy get home, and make sure there ain't any worms in your pockets and no flowers in that hair of yours."

Eddie giggles and giggles, not paying any mind to his mama's warnings. How can he? His chums are waiting. He has given just about every flower a name, and any worm that slithers across his path has a friend for life.

Eddie is a baby with stars in his big brown eyes, big brown eyes that are open windows to a soul full of sweet, cottony dreams.

"That's one sweet, beautiful little boy you got there, Lahteese," everyone always says.

However, the problem with sweetness is—everything and everybody wants some. Who doesn't like a cool sweet lick of ice cream, a ripe cherry, or spicy tea with a touch of honey? And even sweeter than that is a beautiful little boy with stars for eyes and cotton candy for a soul.

Eddie sometimes wanders a little farther than his boundaries and plays nearer to the gate on his parents' four acres of land. He loves the extra-green grass there, and waves at every passing truck and zip-zipping little car on Highway 51. As the jonquils sway back and forth, he just sits there and plays while all his neighbor-mamas, as he calls them, wave at him and his neighbor-daddies give him a honk.

§

Further down the road, Trais Johnson steps off a Greyhound bus. His eyes blink out the Carbondale sun. The earth tightens beneath his heaviness, and groans at his closed soul. Big, tall, strong, and broad, with every step his muscles ache, his legs are stiff, and his arms need moving.

Honk, honk. "Over here, Nephew!" His aunt yells while getting out of her white, pristine Malibu with the license plate that reads: MZPRISC. "C'mon over here. I done made you some smothered chicken and iced tea. Let's go get it," she says while placing a fallen hair back into position.

Trais smiles at the thought of his mother's sister's smothered chicken— her gravy just-the-right-brown and perfectly seasoned. The chicken, spicy and sweet with a tad of pure maple syrup, and all of it poured generously over a bed rice. "Emm, emm, here I come, Auntie!"

When he gets to her, he throws down his bag and picks her up.

"Put me down, 'fore you wrinkle my clothes," she says laughing loudly.

"Boy, you sho'll is getting grown—and handsome too. Look at my big sister's boy!"

Trais lifts her up and down a few times before he puts her on the ground. "Auntie Kaynisha, you looking good too, and if I recall correctly you done losta few pounds, aintcha?" He teases.

Kaynisha gives her nephew a hush, and pokes one of his muscles. "Been working out, huh?"

Trais laughs and mistakenly coughs in her face. "Oooh, Auntie, I'm sorry. Listen, before you even get started, I picked up some cough medicine before I got on the bus," he says while picking up his bag.

Kaynisha shoots him an arched eyebrow and a twisted pair of lips then says, "Yeah. OK, just make sure you take some more when we get in the house, 'cause that sounds awful."

After a few more hugs, Kaynisha says, "Okay, let's go."

Trais and Kaynisha get in the car. Her automobile is jasmine-scented. The seats and carpet have not one crumb. The dashboard shines. Even the windows are clean.

Trais says to his aunt, "You clean this car every time you get in it or some-thing?"

Kaynisha laughs and says, "Just about." She stops laughing and sighs before continuing. "Trais, me and your mom grew up in dust and disorder. Our house and everything and everyone in it was so dysfunctional. I can't stand messiness and grime, it reminds me too much of my childhood."

Trais watches the trees pass through his reflection as they serenely move toward her quaint and tidy forest-green house that sits ever so cutely in a woodsy alcove that looks like God made it just for her.

Kaynisha asks, "So, we've both got something new. I've got my new house, and you're seventeen. So, how is it?"

Trais gives his aunt a corrective look, and says, "Auntie, look at me. My muscles are so defined, my striations so deep, I look more twenty-one than seventeen," he says, kissing his biceps.

"Boy, puhleeze," Kaynisha says. "Now answer my question."

"It's cool," Trais replies, unexcited.

"You are still keeping busy, aren't you?" Kaynisha asks, concerned. "You know idle hands are the devil's workshop."

Trais quickly answers, "No, Auntie, everything's going well. I'm still in Jazz band, football, ROTC, and the drama club. I'm good. Trust me."

The answer satisfies her so she moves on. "How's your mother, how's Tina?" Kaynisha asks.

"Mama's fine. She's still here and there. She calls sometimes. Last I heard from her, she called from a hospital in Iowa. From what I can tell now, she's taking her meds, so she's okay. She talks about you all the time, 'My baby sister this, my baby sister that.' When I told her you bought a house. She was so happy."

Kaynisha's sister's illness has never been easy for her to talk about. She changes the subject. "So, Nephew, what made you decide to finally come spend a summer with me? I'm happy you're here. You know that. But…is everything alright?"

Trais gives a big manly laugh, so deep it makes Kaynisha look at him twice.

"Auntie, I just decided to come spend the summer with you. You know spend some time with my favorite aunt. Most of the people I spend my time with ain't family, and I've been staying at my friends' houses more and more, so I'm switching that up a bit."

After a moment of quiet, Kaynisha says, "Well, listen, I bought a house in Anna. Do you know where that is? Do you know what that means?"

Trais gives his aunt a sly look and says, "Yes. I know, Auntie. I looked it up. *Sundown Towns*, James something, right?"

Kaynisha let's out a big laugh of her own, "Boy," she says, "you're as sharp as your mother. Yeah, the author's name is James Loewen. Anyway, I live there and a few more of us do too. Just be sure when you go out without me that you're minding your manners, okay. The same way you do when you're at your grandparents, with their picky selves, just take it easy and be patient with folks."

Kaynisha starts honking the horn looking out the window and waving excitedly.

"Auntie, who you honking and waving at, the trees?"

"Nah, boy. You don't see my little neighbor over there sitting in the grass? That's my lil' Eddie."

Kaynisha yells out the window, "Hey, baby muffin! Hey, Eddie!"

"Oh, I see him now. He is a little one. Hmm. And he's cute too," Trais says.

The comment swirls in Kaynisha's mind. It alerts something distant and unimaginable within her.

Instantly, Trais realizes his mistake and blurts out, "Yeah, Auntie, I've been working with the kids in the youth groups. You know teaching the grammar-school kids football and stuff."

His response righted and dismissed his comment altogether, made it rational, so Kaynisha got back to enjoying time with her nephew without another thought about it.

§

Moon. Bright Morning Sun.

Bright and extra early, this full-of-shine morning, Baby Eddie runs down the hill with a belly full of biscuits and his mama calling after him.

"Yes, mama, I know. I will not put worms in my pocket," he yells running down the hill out of his mama's sight.

"Watch'm Jingles and LuLu," Lahteese says as she lets her husband's two lazy yet territorial hounds out of their pen. They look at her with their big tired eyes, then take off with just enough speed to get there next Sunday morning.

Just short of a mile away, Trais kisses his sleeping aunt and tells her he is going outside to enjoy the sun and take a look at her land.

"So you're finally taking off without me, huh?" Kaynisha asks. "Well, up the road is the Reddings. Feel free to walk up there and introduce yourself. Oh, yeah. There's a park and a field house not far from their house either. People tend to just leave all kinds of sports equipment in there. You can use anything you want, just don't break it and put it back exactly like you found it."

Trais kisses his aunt goodbye and walks onto the porch. He stretches his long, thick limbs. His muscles, sinewy and full, tight and gorgeous, flex in the sun. His brown skin is marvelous.

He jumps off the porch and walks and walks. He admires the quiet massiveness of the land. Whistling Vivaldi, he walks on. The sound of his being causes the grasshoppers and crickets to scatter.

Suddenly, he hears something. He squints his eyes, scans the landscape. In the distance, he sees the faintest glimmer of a shining low-cropped afro. He peers intently and draws connections. His mind works. *The neighbor,* he thinks.

Trais quickens his pace. Eddie is standing where the grass is tallest. Behind Eddie the trees are dense, the ground is dark from their canopy. The Redding's house sits far in the distance.

After a few minutes of staring intently at him, Trais captures Baby Eddie's attention.

Eddie smiles and waves exuberantly.

Trais looks at all the grass surrounding Eddie then down at the concrete beneath his own feet before responding. "Hi," he intentionally says in a low voice while waving excitedly and smiling.

Eddie continues playing, but notices that Trais is still standing there. So, Eddie looks up and says, "Would you like to play?"

Trais pretends not to be able to hear him, and gestures for him to come closer.

Eddie walks over to Trais with two fat worms in his little open hands, he says, "Sir, this one's Clemmie, and this one is Ella. Would you like to hold one of 'em?"

Trais reaches for the worm but is still too far; he doesn't move his feet.

Eddie, happy to have someone to play with, walks closer to Trais.

Trais looks down at the concrete, both of their feet are there. Then, he says, "Sure."

With Eddie standing near him, Trais feels an overwhelming warmth. His emotions are balmy and rippling and feathering within him. They flutter around his mouth and flush his cheeks. An intoxicating heat gathers in his palms, and he opens his left hand.

Eddie puts the long, skinny worm into the center of Trais's palm. "Okay, be careful. Her name is Clemmie," he says.

Trais lets the worm rest in his hand. The wriggling chill provides just enough frost to unhinge the heat and pressure that shut his jaws. He asks Eddie, "You're nice. What's your name?"

Lahteese and Vollmer Redding's sweet little boy tells Trais his name, his nickname, phone number, and address without pausing to take a breath.

"Well, you certainly are a smart little boy," Trais says stroking Eddie's glistening brown hair with one hand, and gingerly holding Clemmie with the other.

Eddie feels comforted under his touch. Trais's large hand feels strong like his daddy's. Eddie misses his dad. Vollmer isn't home nowhere near as much as he used to be. His job as a regional truck driver has made their once dependable daily daddy-son dates sporadic. Eddie thinks back to the days he used to spend with him. The nights he laid cradled in his arms. The smell of his father's shirts, the sound of his dad's voice saying, "I love you." Just the thought of Vollmer's voice makes Eddie close his eyes. He savors the memory; without thinking, he snuggles against Trais.

Eddie's head resting against Trais's leg causes Trais's breath to catch in his chest. Awful feelings tear open inside him—desires surge through his entire body.

Trais remembers the last time he even came close to feeling this way. It was when a young mother, who had more groceries than hands, asked if he would watch her daughter as she got the rest of her items on the bus.

Trais said, "Sure," while looking at the small, timid girl who looked to be about three and the empty seats all around them.

When the mother sat her child beside Trais and walked up the aisle and off the bus to collect her things from the bust stop bench, Trais acted as if he was dusting something off his pants and placed his hand on the little girl's thigh. When he looked down into the shock and fear that was in her eyes, a nefarious joy detonated. He quickly told her, "do not make a sound," and rubbed her genitalia until tears began forming in her eyes.

As soon as the mom got back on the bus, Trais rushed past her and jumped off.

The last thing Trais heard before running down the alley was the bus driver's voice shouting, "Hey, get back here!"

From that time to the present moment, Trais has rubbed, squeezed, and fondled any child unlucky enough to be alone with him.

Returning his thoughts to Eddie, Trais begins massaging Baby Eddie's neck and stroking his cheek.

The crickets all chirp at once, screaming with their legs.

Trais's overly-warm, sweaty palm makes Eddie uncomfortable. All at once it dawns on Eddie, nothing about the tall, hairless, unusually affectionate man reminds him of his daddy.

A mournful, cold feeling ices through Eddie's abdomen and great, heavy blocks of terror fill his arms and legs. Eddie wants to scream but dread has clenched his airway. He is paralyzed. He wants to grab Clemmie and run, but he can't. His eyes, wide and wet, stare at Trais.

Trais sees the change in Eddie's mood and behavior, and the intense repulsion in his eyes.

Trais bends down on one knee, puts his face in front of Eddie's, and falsely asks, "What's wrong?" But, Trais knows what is wrong. He's seen Eddie's expression countless times before. He's had the expression himself on more occasions than he can remember. Based on his own experiences, Trais also knows that Eddie will not fight nor flight, but freeze.

Eddie can't speak. He's frozen in fear.

Trais says, "Eddie, don't be afraid. I'm your friend. C'mon, let's just keep playing. Everything is alright." Trais feigns interest in Clemmie. He pretends to talk to the worm and pretends the worm is talking back to him. "Okay, you hold Clemmie and let me listen," Trais says.

Baby Eddie agrees.

Trais giggles. Eddie relaxes. Trais laughs. Eddie laughs uncontrollably. As the worm wriggles from Trais's palm to Eddie's then back again, Eddie loses himself in the beauty and wonder of his childhood.

The worm wriggles and wriggles as Trais inches closer and closer to Eddie. In a moment, Trais's face is intentionally just a turn of the neck away from Eddie's lips.

And when the planned inevitable happens, Eddie's vision goes black, and water breaks from him. Fear, innocence, and youth pour downward onto the ground in long streams down his thighs and from his eyes. Life as sweet, precious Eddie knows it leaves his mind and body in one terrible scream.

A scream that bounces off the concrete, skips along the grass, climbs up the bark, jumps from leaf to leaf, rides the air, and squeezes itself beneath the cracked window of the Redding kitchen.

Startled, having lost his sense of control, Trais reacts impulsively. He reflexively, mistakenly, hits Eddie on the head. Baby Eddie falls backward into the grass hard. The crickets scream.

Trais gazes at Eddie lying quietly, not moving. The vile impulses surge. Trais's eyes sees only what he finds desirable. He falls forward, feverishly kisses Eddie's mouth, and fondles his small body wildly.

The crickets screeeeam hard with their legs. The dogs howl. Trais can hear their presence coming—beating down faster and faster, closer and closer. He roughly handles Eddie one last time before running completely out of sight.

§

The hounds lick Eddie's still face. The crickets' legs cool with inactivity.

"Baby! Eddie!" Lahteese yells. Her legs running, hard and fast, toward the cling-a-ling of the dogs' metal ID tags.

"Eddie!" Lahteese prays and runs, prays and runs. Lulu barks. "Eddie!"

Lahteese can see the tops of the dogs' behinds, their tails waving stiffly in the air. "Eddie! Oh, dear God."

She slides part of the way on her knees to her baby. She touches his face, looks at the mark on his head, puts her ear on his chest to check if his heart is beating.

She rubs his arms vigorously. He doesn't move.

She looks at him to be sure she sees all his injuries before picking him up.

She stalls suddenly. His shorts are wet.

The elastic of his little blue shorts is twisted. The center seam is pulled to the left. The band of the elastic is dirty on the inside. There are small welts on his tender skin. She smells urine. She sees his little socks and shoes are drenched. There are tears on his face.

She looks around her, looks back down at her child, looks around again, remembers the way she came in and tries to see if any other tracks exist. She sees nothing but notices that the very place she is sitting is flat. The grass is lying on its side.

She takes off her apron, and wraps it around her child quickly and carefully. Lahteese holds Baby Eddie close to her and rushes home.

§

Two cars come up the road in a cloud of dust. The women hurry toward the Redding's door, and the men help them inside.

The medics had already restored Eddie's consciousness and bandaged his wound.

Eddie's maternal and paternal grandmothers, Florene and Myrtle, call his name softly.

He opens his eyes and smiles.

"Your granddaddy and your pawpaw here too, Eddie," says his paternal grandfather Harold. His maternal grandfather, Albert, grabs his little hand into his and waves.

"I heard you played possum, boy, when they found you. You remembered us teaching you that when we hunting, huh?"

Eddie smiles real big; that's his little way of saying "yes" when he has a splitting headache.

Florene, a retired nurse asks Eddie, "Grandbaby, I ain't gone bug you, but I got to know something because my friends are coming to take you for a check-up, and I need to know what to tell'em. You sure you weren't unconscious? If you were playing possum, why didn't you say something when your mother grabbed you?"

Eddie starts to cry and says, "Grandma, I thought mama wasn't real. I thought I was dreaming." Well, baby, why didn't you open "Yes, Ma'am," Eddie replies.

Myrtle runs from the room with her hand over her mouth, her husband Harold chases her.

Albert grabs Eddie's hand, nudges his wife to the side, and says, ""Son, you alright? Your head isn't hurting you too bad is it?"

Eddie responds, "No…well, emm hmm, a little."

"That's okay, son," his voice faltering. "Your granny's friends, Twan and John, are replacing the medics that were here before. You remember those guys. They taught you how to play basketball. They're gonna get you all fixed up, okay."

"Yes, sir."

Florene settles the logistics with Lahteese. She tells her Eddie's physician has been paged and he will join her former team at the hospital.

Lahteese breaks down twice during the telling. Then, she asks Eddie's grandparents to go with him. She says, "I need y'all to take Eddie so I can help the police, if need be. More than that, I just can't imagine," her tears swell, her chest rises and falls, "anybody else telling Eddie's daddy this."

"You haven't told Vollmer yet?" her mother asks.

"No, Myrtle." Lahteese's father says, "she's doing right. She tell Vollmer that while he's out there on that road, that boy'll surely run that truck into every ditch, and up every light pole from wherever he is to here."

As the paramedics prepare Eddie to be transported, the grandmothers balk at their haste. "Be quick, but be gentle," Grandma Florene hisses.

The grandmothers cannot be talked down from riding in the ambulance.

Grandpa Albert says, "C'mon Harold, ride with me."

Everyone gathers into their respective vehicles.

Harold solemnly looks at the late morning sun and watches the lights of the ambulance whirl. He listens to the siren scream and remembers Eddie's face, and bangs his fist hard and steady against the dashboard. Albert stops the car and just looks at Harold's fist slamming into the dashboard.

The leather pops with each whack.

Albert covers his face with his hands and cries. Their pain together equals a century of experiences of all kinds—deaths, heartaches, and injustice—but nothing, nothing has ever pained them, hurt their lives, and made them question their God like this.

§

Late Morning Sun.

From a distance, traveling down the familiar winding road that leads to his house, Vollmer sees two extra cars in his driveway. *Ah, our parents are here,* he thinks, smiling excitedly. He admires the sunlight covering the field, shining down on the house, making the grass sheen.

He sees the police officers coming down the road, but he doesn't think twice about it. His mother is famous for making pies and cookies for the officers. The entire force loves and respects her. *Hmm. They must've heard she was here,* he figures. As usual, he just gives them a wave and keeps moving. He doesn't notice the disturbed look on each of their faces.

Vollmer walks in his house, smiles broadly, and announces, "Hey, hey! I'm so glad to see all of you. What a nice surprise!"

He is so delighted to see them that the somberness of their mood doesn't register. He goes and gives his mother his signature tickle under her arm.

She doesn't even smile, let alone gush into giggles the way she usually does. "Alright everybody, what's wrong?" Vollmer says while looking around the room. He thinks, *The house is in order, all my loved ones are here—where's my son?* Panic takes over his mood, "Where's my boy?" Vollmer nervously asks.

Lahteese speaks up. "Vollmer, just wait a minute. Sit down first, honey."

Vollmer's eyes swell. His hands get big. "Nah, just wait a minute nothing. Where's my boy?" He asks, losing his cool.

Vollmer's daddy steps in and says, "Son, please. Please sit down. Eddie's in the back room. He's sleeping. We need to tell you something, but you need to sit down first."

Vollmer looks into his father's eyes and sees something he has never ever seen before. It wasn't there when their house was completely consumed by fire, or when his brother died. He looks around the room, looks into each of their faces and realizes that whatever this thing is, it is beyond sad, beyond the normal hum-drum, and goes beneath the regular turmoils of life. The thought of it, the thought of whatever it is drains him. He drops his attitude, goes over to the chair that's been pulled out for him, and sits down next to his standing wife.

"Somebody molested our son, Vollmer."

Vollmer asks, "What did she say?" He heard the words, understood them, then didn't. Lahteese reluctantly repeats herself.

Everybody's anguish ignites freely this time. They've been holding it at a simmer all day. Now, the feelings blaze and boil.

Baby Eddie's daddy shudders and shakes and runs down the hall to his son's room. His father and father-in law apprehend him. "No!" They whisper. "Not like this. Calm down first. You'll just further upset him." They walk him back to the living room and sit him in the chair.

Vollmer falls on his knees and hollers, "Who did it?!" Lahteese explains they don't know yet; however, the police have been working all morning and are still searching this afternoon.

Vollmer sends his fist diving into the floor and yells, "My God!" The men help him to his feet. The women cry.

Vollmer stands up and looks at the pictures of his son on the walls: Eddie's kindergarten graduation, his first cupcake, his birthday at the beach, Eddie asleep on his mother's chest. "He's just a baa-by!"

Overcome by anger, Vollmer runs for his son's room again. Albert and Harold have to run to catch him. They grab him. His father says, "He's sleeping. Please let him rest. Plus, he doesn't need to see you like this. It will upset him."

Vollmer allows them to walk him back, but his arms are bonfires. His legs are flames. "Not my boy! Not my son! Father in heaven! God have mercy!" He punches the walls. His anger is embers in his bones; it flares a rage that burns his skin. He cries to put it out. He punches the wall again and again to transfer the pain. Everyone cries. Then, he turns his anger against his wife. Where were you, Lahteese?! Why weren't you watching our son?!

The questions break her heart.

Lahteese calmly says to Vollmer, "Husband, you know I love our baby more than life itself. I was here, Vollmer. He was playing in the field where he always plays. I was here. I was cleaning and baking. The dogs were out. I don't know what happened. No one knows what happened."

Both Lahteese's and Vollmer's parents go to Lahteese and hold her.

Vollmer's father says to him, "Now, son, you know your wife love that boy of yours. That's why you married her, 'cause you knew she'd be a great mother. This ain't no time to be turning on each other."

Vollmer hangs his head, walks over to his family, and they all embrace.

§

Shortly after they arrived home from the hospital, two hours before Vollmer came in, Baby Eddie's paternal grandmother stuffed short pieces of cotton that she had prayed over into his ears. She knew his father would explode when he found out what happened, and she did not want Baby Eddie to hear his father coming apart.

Even in his sleep, with the cotton in his ears, Baby Eddie could make out his father's voice.

Baby Eddie pulls the cotton out of his ears and hears his daddy and what sounds like his whole family crying. Eddie sits on the side of his bed for a minute. His daddy's pain makes him feel unsure. He thinks about what to do. He wipes his eyes, looks at the tears in his hands, and remembers the day his uncle John died.

Eddie envisions how sad his daddy was, how his daddy didn't feel better until the preacher sang. Eddie searches his mind for the words, then distinctly recalls that he'd been taught them. A smile covers his little lips. He clearly sees the June day when his daddy, Uncle John, Papa Harold, and Papa Albert were standing around the grill singing the same song the preacher sang at Uncle John's funeral. He remembers how the grannies joined in, and when his mama brought out the potato salad, she sang too. He chuckles when he recalls his daddy picking him up for the encore. And that's where he learned the hymn, "His Eye Is On The Sparrow," right there in his daddy's arms.

Eddie wipes his face, stands up on his little feet, and walks straight out into the living room. When everybody stops and looks at him, he opens his tiny mouth and sings just the way his daddy taught him.

§

Phones ring. Women's and men's voices exchange tidbits of information. "Did you hear that?" "I think that screaming came from the Redding's place." "I did see the police leaving from up there." "I think something happened over by the field."

Kaynisha hangs up the phone and goes to check on Trais. "Hey, Trais," she says, walking toward his bedroom with a freshly made sandwich atop a blue saucer. "Did you hear or see anything strange when you were out today? I heard something might have happened over at one of my neighbor's houses."

Kaynisha almost drops the saucer when she sees her nephew. The light from the hallway slices through his room and shines on his partially naked body. He is sitting on the floor in the darkest corner of the room. She walks over to him. "Nephew, what's wrong with you?" Trais's legs are drawn up to his chest. His eyes are streaming. "Trais, what happened?"

He doesn't say anything.

Kaynisha puts the saucer down and seats herself on the corner of the bed nearest to Trais. She sits with him, saying nothing for several minutes. She rubs his head, massages his shoulders. Then, tells him about the day he was born, and how happy she was, how she's known him for all his life and how nothing will ever make her stop loving him. She shares with him some of the information she's been learning in, and her experiences from, her atypical psychology and pathological processes courses. She tells him, "studying people from all over the world, with every problem you can think of, and some you can't imagine, has taught me to be helpful, open-minded and accepting of others in ways I thought I never could be."

Trais says nothing.

"Trais, what is it?" she asks him again. She waits, then encourages him, "Nephew, I'm your aunt. I care about you. I love you. We only got eleven years between us, whatever you're going through, I've probably been through it too. I can help you."

Trais's aunt's words are a balm to his troubled soul. For so long, he's felt burdened by the weight of his secrets. He thinks about it: Kaynisha has always been so nice to him; she's been his best friend, his sister, his aunt, and sometimes his mother too. The thought of sharing this thing that has been gnawing at him and taking over his life makes him feel both heavier and lighter. Trais rubs his head and begins to cry. For some reason, in this moment, sitting in his aunt's house, he feels more reflective and conscious than ever. A sense of guilt begins growing in him as he looks at the *Bible* sitting on the nightstand and the black Serenity Prayer decal that has been smoothly applied onto her cool, gray accent wall.

The breaking point comes when Kaynisha places her hand on Trais's head and says, "Give it to God, Trais. He will see you through."

Trais can no longer hold back. He puts his forehead on his knees, wraps his arms tighter around his legs, and tells his aunt he is too outdone, too disheartened and distraught to carry the evils of his life any further. Without stopping to second guess himself, he tells her exactly what he did to Baby Eddie.

His words sicken her. "Oh Lord," she hisses. She wants to take her fists and beat him, beat him away from the devilment, beat him back into right thinking, beat him back into the nephew she knew. But she cannot hurt him, everything inside of her makes her want to hit him, the same way her father used to hit her mother, the same way her mother hit her, but she cannot not bring herself to do it. He is her nephew, the youngest son of her only sister and she knows that if she finds a reason to raise her hand to hit him, she'll find reasons from now on to become the worst parts of her mother and father. She has never wanted that kind of life for herself, so she bites her lip hard, so hard that it bleeds.

"Why? Trais, why?" She screams as blood stains her teeth and seeps into the folds of her gum line.

"I don't know, Auntie. I'm sick. It's like something inside me takes over."

She looks into his face and in that moment sees her sister and all the things that remind her of Tina—all of the drugs, the bad choices, the men, the countless mood swings. Kaynisha tells Trais, "I remember when your mom and I were just children. I was only eight. Tina was thirteen. I remember asking her, 'What's wrong with you, Tina?'

You see, when she came out the bathroom, she was crying a little bit; shortly afterward, our old lowdown uncle came out of there too. At the time, I didn't quite understand what was going on, but I knew our uncle had no business in the bathroom with either one of us, especially while we were bathing. I remember Tina crying all through the night that night. After that, life was not the same."

Trais completely astonished says, "Uncle Reyvin touched my mama?"

Kaynisha ashamed to admit it, explains to Trais that their uncle touched a lot of women and girls. He was a known womanizer and as he got older he became known as someone you did not want to leave your daughters around. Then, Kaynisha begins to cry. She says, "Trais, that was the first time that I knew of that something happened to Tina, but it was not the last. After Reyvin started raping her, she became very depressed. She would sit alone in her room in the dark, even on the weekends, even when it was nice out, she would just sit in there."

Trais asks, angry as hell, "Why didn't someone do something? Where was grandma? Where was grandpa?"

Kaynisha says without blinking, "Your grandfather has always been a very closed off person. He has never really cared for anything or anybody. He provided for mama and us, but that's about it. He was there and not there, Trais. Honestly, the way daddy and Reyvin turned out, I am certain that they were abused. And my mother, God bless her heart, to this day she still stuck in time. Even back then, she was no more mentally prepared than us kids were. She's been traumatized by her own abuse. She remains in deep denial of everything. She's never been able to believe anything she doesn't wanna see. But, Trais, you know me and you know I love my sister. Once, I knew what was going on, after Tina finally told me, I pulled a knife on that rascal and told him if he ever touch my sister again I was gon' kill him, daddy, and mama. I was screaming and hollin' so loud that the neighbors came to the door. That night, he was left. I didn't hear nothing else about him, 'til they found him dead down there in Louisiana."

Trais rocks back and forth, clenches his fist, and grinds his teeth. He growls, "Tell me the rest."

Kaynisha tells her nephew one of her most painful memories. She recalls the day her mother called her high school and told her vis phone: "I need you to come home now and babysit your nephew. Tina is not treating Trais right. She act like she love him one minute then hate him the next. I need you to come home now, so I can take her to the doctor, 'fore she hurt this child."

Although Kaynisha tried, she could not find the words to describe to Trais how stunned and confused Tina's actions left her. But being the good sister she's always been, from that day forth she did her best to care for Tina and Trais as best a fourteen-year-old with dreams of getting far away from the craziness of her childhood could.

Trais screams, "I have always felt my mama loves me, but doesn't like me. Did she treat my older brother the same way? Is that why he never comes around?"

Kaynisha puts his head on her lap, and tells him everything he never heard before. She tells him how Charles, Tina's first child, Trais's oldest brother, was the lucky one because his father's family took him from Tina when he was just three days old. She explains to Trais that Charles's father and Tina met while they were both hospitalized. After his family confirmed that their son had fathered Tina's baby, they immediately took action to obtain full custody and parental rights.

Kaynisha says, "Charles was not allowed contact with our side of the family until he was fifteen years old and even then he could only call and write. Tina had him when she was fourteen. I know you did not know any of this because our family is so secretive and everyone always lies about Tina's age. But she had him at fourteen and got pregnant with you at nineteen. Because Tina been in and out of mental hospitals most of her life, people have never been able to put two and two together about her."

Kaynisha pauses for a moment, takes a deep breath, then continues, "So, when Tina would come home from her stints in the hospital, and would return to school, she'd tell people she was younger than she was. I did not think much of it because I felt she was already dealing with so much and I figured she was just embarrassed to be four and five years older than everyone else. Then, when she got pregnant with you, and I had heard it was by a freshman. I nearly slapped her myself 'cause that meant she was nineteen messing with a fourteen/fifteen-year-old boy, and, if you ask me, well on her way to becoming Uncle Reyvin."

Kaynisha looks down upon Trais's face and sees deep pain. She says to him, to break up some of the awfulness of the moment, "After she had Charles and Reyvin got put in jail for domestic battery, Tina was okay for a few years. She attended high school regularly. She was doing okay. She was dressing different, talking different. I would even see her just sitting in the park talking with people. She was particularly fond of chatting with this kid she called J-Mac. They would just sit and talk about everything, TV, the news, music. I could tell he liked her after a while. I think she knew it too, because I noticed she stopped going to the park after he started getting all googly eyed. Anyway, if my memory serves me correctly, she was doing good for about a year then when she stopped going to the park, something else started happening." Then, Kaynisha got quiet again.

Trais says to her, "Go on, Auntie."

Kaynisha says, "Well, one day I saw her with this girl named Jaymel."

Kaynisha noticed that when she mentioned Jaymel, Trais's body stiffened and his breathing became erratic. She pauses for a moment then continues to see if more details will bring out whatever Jayme's name is invoking.

"Yeah, all of a sudden they were real good friends. But one day, they just stopped hanging out. Another friend of ours said that Jaymel told Tina something that messed her all up, but I never found out what it was. Shortly after that your mom slipped completely back into that darkness, and from what I can see, she's never really bounced back." She sighs then says, "Next thing I knew, Tina was in repeat mode. She was pregnant, promiscuous, and had started smoking marijuana again. Then, she took off. After that, she was back and forth back and forth."

Trais rolls off of his aunt's lap and places his hands over his face. "Auntie," he said, his voice shaking, "I know Jaymel."

Kaynisha's eyes widen. "How do you know her?"

"I was hanging out over at her place when I was in sixth grade. A bunch of us would go over there."

Kaynisha, nervous, afraid of the answer asks, "What were y'all doing?"

Trais says, "At first, we were trying to help her find her husband. After she couldn't find him she kinda started getting real attached to me."

"Trais" Kaynisha says, "she's your mother's age."

"I know, Auntie, but Jaymel ain't nothing like mama; she's fun and she liked being with me. To me, she's cool, older, but cool, just a older version of her daughter, and all us was cool with Queena; we all went to school together. I didn't really know Queena well or nothing, we really didn't talk much, 'cause she and my boy were doing their thing, but I still hung out over there because I was with him."

Trais took a moment to think about what he said, and why he felt so drawn to Jaymel even though he knew he felt something was not right about being with her. He thinks of all the times his mother fiercely refused to show him any affection, how she acted like it repulsed her to touch him. He thinks about all the confusion he's held and never voiced, how he knows his mother loves him, but never hugs him or kisses him or is tender with him. He thinks about how he's hated her for that. And he thinks about how that made him weak against Jaymel's advances.

Kaynisha stands up and says, "Nephew, tell me exactly what she did to you. I can tell by the look on your face something that wasn't supposed to happen happened."

Trais tells his aunt how Jaymel, on his eleventh birthday, showed him her breasts. She said it was his present. And how she'd make him touch her between her legs and how she would kiss him all over his body.

When Trais remembers Jaymel kissing him, he remembered how she begged and begged him to put his lips against hers. How she looked like she was about to cry if he did not do it. Then, he remembers how he felt with Baby Eddie, it was that same kind of intensity, that same level of sick want. Thoughts shuffle like cards in Trais's mind. He connects all of the things that have happened to him to what he did to Eddie. He stands up, grabs his clothes and shoes, and shouts, "Auntie, you've got to get me out of here. I have to get some help."

Kaynisha says, "I know, Trais, I know."

He sees her wondering. "Auntie, just call the police."

The very mention of police causes both of them to take a deep breath.

Kaynisha feels as if her heart is freezing in her chest. Neither of them can envision him being in jail.

They sit in silence. Trais removes his phone from his pocket. "I'll call them," he says. He dials 9. At that precise moment, Kaynisha, for some reason, remembers watching the *Color Purple*. As clear as a bell, she hears Sofia say, "I had to fight my daddy. I had to fight my uncles. I had to fight my brothers." Then, the scene, the scene with the white sheriff appears all around her. She sees the sheriff cold-cock Sofia, knocking her flat on her back, dust flying, underclothing exposed. That's exactly how Kaynisha feels right now. She feels that all the men who ever took from her, her sister, their mother, she felt that the evil spirits that dwelt in them were rising up and coming to take her nephew too.

Just one moment before Trais presses send, she snatches the phone out his hand and says, "The police won't be much help in getting your spirit restored and your behavior corrected. All the men and women who ever hurt our family had the police called on'em at one time or another, and I wish I could say that the help they provided was anything more than a temporary break from the madness they never stopped causing."

Trais ponders her words. He remembers the many faces he's seen through the years that started out bright and full of life that ended up tattooed and filled with death. He remembers hearing about the prison industrial complex, the jail rapes, the school to prison pipeline, and he remembers swearing he would never let that happen to him. He resolves in his heart that he needs help, but he also knows that being in jail without the proper support will likely make him worse, not better.

Kaynisha explains her decision. She tells Trais how his great-grandfather left in and out of town his entire life evading angry women and fathers, and how the police would put him away and soon as he got out, he'd be right back at it. "He needed a support group and good strong righteous men to hold him accountable," she says. "You need that too, Trais." Kaynisha closes her eyes, puts her hand over her heart, and decides she's going to try and get her nephew the type of help the other troublesome men in her family never had. "Trais, I want you to see Dr. Margis, first. She'll be certain that you get the treatment you need, get you into a small group, and possibly into residential care. Margis has a clinic that focuses on legal, mental, and spiritual counseling. You need spiritual counseling more than anything. But, promise me, if I get you to her, you'll tell the truth, you'll tell her exactly what happened and you'll do exactly as she tells you to do. Let her and her team deliver you to the police, that way you'll get the support you need."

"Yes, Auntie, I will. I promise," Trais says fervently, sincerely.

Kaynisha gets up and says, "Okay, let me make a few phone calls." She stops suddenly. And yells, "Wait! Trais! You do know what you did is wrong, right? You know you hurt that little boy and his family? You know they'll never be the same again, don't you?"

Trais replies, "Yes. Auntie, I know."

Kaynisha turns completely away from the phone and continues, "Trais, really, you can't do that ever again. You have to stop it. Children are not sexual objects; they're not to be touched in a sexual manner. One of my favorite teachers, Professor Telayo, told me, 'Sexual abuse changes a child at the molecular level, forever altering the child's personality.' She said, 'For most abused children, feelings of humiliation and worthlessness haunt them for the rest of their lives.' And Trais, it has been well-documented that more than half of the women and girls who get involved in prostitution, who also have alcohol and drug addictions, were sexually abused as children and the same goes for men and boys. When people abuse children, just one time, can ruin their lives forever. Forever! And for those that don't get caught in street life, for many of them, the pain of their abuse stalks them to the day they leave this earth. A lot of the men and women from the case studies we've researched in class, report that they are still deeply hurting from things that happened to them thirty, forty years ago. The aftershock is devastating and long lasting, sexual problems, marital problems, low self-esteem, suicidal ideation—the destruction never stops."

Trais nods.

Kaynisha persists, "Trais, you have to take responsibility for what you have done. What you did today isn't Jaymel's fault, or your mother's fault, or your uncle's fault—what you did today was entirely you. Your family history may leave you susceptible to certain things, but it is up to you to control your behavior. You can control this. You have the power. Do you understand me?"

Trais answers, "Okay, Auntie."

Kaynisha, determined to make Trais face his actions, questions him and asks him to see himself in his behavior. She asks, "Trais, tell me the part you played in making today what it was?"

Trais nervously looks around. He has never seen his aunt so assertive. He quivers a bit and nervously says, "Well, I was there, and I did what I did."

Kaynisha, careful to not become too emotional, says in an even, measured tone, "Nephew, you have to give me a better answer than that. You have to have better answers for yourself. Which of your actions and thoughts brought you here to this moment? Tell me what's been happening in your mind."

Trais gives her a quizzical look and says, "My thought life. Over and over again, like everyday I replay all the things Jaymel and I used to do. Although I was afraid and nervous when it first started happening, it's like I became addicted to the rush of it all. I've been with a few girls my own age and even some older, but nothing gave me that rush I felt with Jaymel; you know, when I was young and afraid. Not, until I started …being her. Oh, God." Trais stops, looks down at his hands, clasps them together, and says through chattering teeth, "Am I pedophile, Auntie? I heard someone screaming at Jaymel one time, calling her a pedophile. She was all drunk and high and stuff. They kept calling her that, then she just said, 'Yeah, I's likes 'em young. So what?'" With that, Trais falls to his knees, inconsolable.

Kaynisha stands him to his feet, "Nah-uh," she says, "This ain't no time to be falling apart. Tell me about your thought life. That's one of the things behind this—that's how these types of behaviors are fed, with thoughts, fantasies."

Trais's face tenses, new tears form, his lips purse and his eyebrows draw together. He mutters, "What?"

"Do you have sexual dreams and fantasies about children?!" she yells.

"Yes. But what does that have to do with anything?"

"A lot, Trais!" Kaynisha screams "That means you're going all the way, so to speak. You're seeing your fantasies through to the very end. That means you're gonna have to break the habit of connecting those thoughts and actions to the very addictive physical pleasure you get when engaging in sexual acts. 'Cause after while, if you don't correct that, the only thing that will turn you on will be those demonic thoughts."

Trais with pure consternation on his face says, "Oh no, that's already started. I used to be cool when I was with my girlfriend. Then after time went by, I had to think about ... well, you know what I had to think about to get it up, you know. But what scared me the most, Auntie, was I used to have to smoke some weed or drink before I...touched a kid, but lately, I don't need to do that at all. I can be straight up sober and in my right mind and do it."

Kaynisha proudly looks at her nephew, tells him he's brave for being so honest, lets him know she's not judging him, and encourages him to go on.

"Well, recently," Trais says, "I been going to chat rooms, watching porn, sexting." In a lower voice he says, "Auntie, I am totally preoccupied by sexual thoughts."

Kaynisha pays attention to the way his voice trails off, and sees a new layer of shame cross his face. She knows that now is the time to give him the hard facts of his actions, while he still has the decency to be ashamed. Kaynisha abruptly says, "Trais, I have this book, it's called *Predators, Pedophiles, Rapists and Other Sex Offenders*. It was written by psychologist Dr. Anna C. Salter. I'll give you a copy. Now, I don't agree with everything written in the book but she made a good point that has stuck with me. She said: 'The cornerstones of [deviant sexual behavior] are distorted thinking and...fantasies. These fantasies play an enormous role in the development of compulsive [deviant sexual behaviors.]' Trais, you see, what happens is this: First, you start out just dreaming and thinking about deviant behaviors; then you start fantasizing and masturbating to them. What people do not generally understand is that masturbation is addictive. It can get ahold of you just like any drug, or alcohol. What makes masturbation especially harmful are the thoughts that accompany it; they progress. Change is inherent to anything that progresses, either it has to be stopped or it will require more. You know how drug addicts talk about having a monkey on their back?"

"Yeah."

"Well, a sex addict does too. The thought life becomes the monkey. Over time, sex addicts require wilder and wilder fantasies to feel their high. What is dangerous about this in your case, or in the case of any person who is a sex offender, is that you are feeding a desire that not only leads to criminal actions, but is also immoral and harmful to all around you."

Trais stands up. "You have my word, Auntie, I don't want what is happening to me to happen to anyone else. Please put me in touch with Margis."

Kaynisha makes the necessary phone calls. She calls Dr. Margis, and tells her that her nephew needs an appointment immediately. Margis agrees to see Trais. Kaynisha makes arrangements to get Trais on the next train out of Carbondale. She schedules him to leave on the 10:15 A.M. Amtrak train that arrives in Chicago at 4 P.M. Dr. Margis says, "I'll pick him up at Union Station."

§

Rain falls in big gloomy drops from the sky. And although it's 10A, it feels like midnight before the funeral. Trais and Kaynisha say all that cannot be said with their faces and body language, with their deep breaths and sad eyes.

As boarding begins, Trais says, "Auntie, thank you."

Tears and raindrops drip one after another from Kaynisha's nose as she pulls the lobe of his ear to her face and tells him, "You're my nephew, Trais, my sister's baby. I can't help but love you. I can't help but help you. But know this, I'm tracking this train, and I'm calling Dr. Margis exactly ten minutes after it arrives, if you're not with her, I'm calling the police. And know this too, nephew,

I will testify against you."

After she let's his ear go, Trais rubs it vigorously and looks at her with fear in his eyes. "Okay," he says with a stutter, "I'll keep my word."

Kaynisha puts Dr. Salter's book in his backpack, grabs his hand, and says, "I'll always love you, no matter what."

§

Kaynisha watches Trais board the train, waves at him until he is no longer in sight, and stands perfectly still, in the spot where he left her, until the rumbling mechanical sounds of the trains can't be heard anymore.

The walk back to her car is tiresome, wearisome, soul-crushing. With Trais gone, her mind focuses clearly, solely on Baby Eddie. Each step she takes is heavy with guilt, grief, confusion. Her stride becomes stumbles. She is careful not to let her feelings overwhelm her before she gets inside.

During her drive home, feelings barge forward. Baby Eddie becomes a pain in her heart. *Dear God,* she thinks. Kaynisha feels every misery from every day of her life eat at the marrow in her bones. She throws up twice before she arrives home.

Six hours after her nephew left, four-o-clock came and went. Dr. Margis looks for Trais, she cannot find him. Kaynisha calls Trais's phone, it goes straight to voice mail. She purposely charged his phone before he left, for this very reason. She gave Trais a picture of Dr. Margis, and text a picture of Trais to her. So she knows there is no logical reason for them not to have connected.

After calling the Reddings and telling them what she knew, and calling the police and telling them all she knew, she unlocked her door, laid on her couch, and took her last breath.

§

The city is warm and noiseless on the Saturday afternoon of July tenth at 4 P.M. Chicago's Union Station, usually abuzz with activity and people at this hour, is uncommonly quiet. Trais walks through the long, wide, shining corridors of the station as if they were the green mile. All morning and afternoon long, for the entire train ride from Carbondale to Chicago, the sound of his aunt's voice, and her admonitions accosted him.

While walking from the train, he still could not believe all that had happened. He pushes through the glass doors and steps into the vestibule. He sees a luxury automobile parked directly across the street; it belongs to Dr. Margis. She is just as Aunt Kaynisha said she would be, stylish haircut, bright feminine clothing, kind eyes. Trais paces in the vestibule. He tugs and squeezes the straps of his backpack as he walks back and forth. *I'm a pedophile*, he thinks and shakes his head.

Dr. Margis checks her watch and opens her car door. "Oh, Auntie Kaynisha, you should've come with me," Trais says aloud to himself as he runs against the wind into the opposite direction of his promise.

§

Out of breath, he stops. He walks to Millennium Park, all along thinking, *I'm A sex offender? A pedophile?* He has considered the same thought so many times his head fills full, congested. He needs a distraction. He takes out his phone and calls his brother.

"Hello," Trais says as he puts his backpack down on the cool, smooth concrete. "Can you hear me?"

"Yeah, I can hear you," his brother Charles says. "Where are you?"

"I'm downtown," Trais says while laying on the ground with his head on his backpack and his arms across his chest.

"Downtown Chicago? I thought you were at Aunt Kaynisha's."

"Yeah, I was, but I'm back here now, hanging out at the bean."

Charles, a bit indignant, says, "You mean the Cloud Gate. I hate when people call it the bean. Calling it the bean will never prompt you to consider how reflection can change perspective."

"Whatever, nerd boy. What's up with you?"

"I'm okay. The question is, what's up with you? You're not supposed to be back for weeks. I know you and Kaynisha are like two peas in a pod. What happened? Is she okay?"

"I just came back early is all. Auntie is fine. Auntie living it up as usual. Ms. Diva." Trais says and coughs loudly.

"Early?" Charles says, not hiding his suspicion. Feeling that he will not get any straight answers, he begins asking more questions. "You still got that stinking cough? That thing sounds even more awful than last time. What did Kaynisha say about it?"

"She just told me to keep an eye on it." Trais sighs deeply and continues, "I'm just calling you to get away for a minute. Why you all on my back?"

Charles, with his suspicions confirmed, pushes a little harder, "Dude, get away from what? Remember who you're talking to. You know I hear everything and infer with the quickness. If you called me, you got something on your mind you need to talk about. Just say it. Don't make me call down there."

Charles's last statement alarms Trais. He had not considered word getting back to Chicago and the ramifications of that. He instantly lightens his mood. "Charles, you know if something was up with Auntie, that whole town would have called up here."

Charles laughs, knowing what Trais was true, and says, "You ain't never lied about that. Okay now, I know, whatever problem you got is yours. Tell me what's going on."

Feeling pressured, near ready to crack, Trais fires back, "Listen man, I'm straight. I just wanted to talk to my brother for a damn minute!"

Charles, never having been one to tolerate disrespect, says coolly and definitely, "I'm done trying to help you. I'll just leave you with a few words of advice, whatever problem you got lil' brother, do not let it fester. Talk to somebody. Seek out wise counsel." Charles then pauses and listens for Trais's reaction.

Trais's mind races, but his lips remain still. He thinks, *tell him about Baby*

Eddie; tell him about being a pedophile. Ask him to go with you to Dr. Margis's. Trais's conscience tries to directs him, but he doesn't comply.

Silence persists past the boundaries of what is sane before Charles speaks again. He says, "Hey, Trais. Dr. King said, 'a time comes when silence is a betrayal.' If something is bothering you and you're not reaching out and getting help—you're betraying yourself." Charles gives Trais a few more seconds, still he says nothing, so he continues, "Okay, well, I hope you have the courage to do the right thing and get yourself whatever help you need. If you need some support or guidance, please find someone to talk to. I don't know why people don't do it more often, but you can just about walk into any church and get help. Now, if that's too much for you, google: 12 step groups, or mental health and your zip code. For real, if you need support though, there are all kinds of Anonymous groups: sex, drugs, alcohol, emotions; you name it, they got it."

Charles pauses again to give his brother some space and time to respond. Trais just breathes.

"Okay, Trais, you better go. I heard a storm's coming. As you carry on with your day, just know, there's nothing new under the sun. No one's so bad off they cannot come back, cannot be redeemed, if they have the will to change."

After another long pause, finally Trais says something, "Hey, Charles. I'm looking in this Cloud Gate thing. You're right, I see a big ball of dark clouds in the distance. You're right about the perspective thing too. I look so small and my shadow it looks so big, big and dark."

Charles sighs. He hears Trais's struggle. But knowing he can do nothing without his cooperation, just bids him farewell. He says, "All right, lil' brother, you better take cover and be safe. I'll be here if you want to come over."

"Okay, maybe I'll see you later," Trais says; both know he's lying.

Charles reassures him anyway and says, "Seriously, if you need me. I'm here."

"I know," Trais says, "Take care. You're a good big brother."

Trais hangs up without saying another word. He stares into Cloud Gate a little longer. He tries to recall what Charles said about Dr. King. It doesn't work.

He tries to think of whether or not he should call his Aunt Kaynisha, but the thought will not stay put long enough for him to make a decision. He looks at the clouds—they look like a gigantic gray army marching above, toward him. He looks back at his own reflection, wrestles with his thoughts, then gives in. A sinister look crosses his face. He picks up his backpack opens it and throws the book his aunt gave him in the trash. His neck sweats. His hips feel oily. Over his shoulder, the small face of a young brown boy is on Crown Fountain. Trais tightens his laces, and gives Cloud Gate one last glance, behind him the brown boy's face frowns. A deeper darkness drifts over Trais's image, it consumes his reflection, fills his mind, then extinguishes the little bit of light that shines between where he's standing and the approaching storm.

§

Trais has been walking the streets of Chicago for three days. This morning he feels especially strange. He's afraid his mind has finally turned into his mother's. He thinks over and over again about Baby Eddie and his dead aunt. When Charles called him a few hours after they spoke and told him his aunt was dead and that the police were looking for him, Trais hung up on him and threw his phone into a dumpster. The weight of his guilt plunged him deep into a state of hallucination inducing unawareness. For two nights, Trais has been slumming from place to place, sleeping here and there. It is clear to anyone who sees him that he is a young man who has completely fallen apart. From the moment he found out his aunt died, he felt in his heart what he'd done had killed her.

Without intention, Trais ends up in the sight of his ex-girlfriend, Charlotte. A girl of inordinate kindness, she was the first person to hear his voice since he'd gone dumb. He tells her about his aunt's death and stopped just short of the reason why he felt she died. Charlotte knows in her spirit, she can discern from the way Trais is speaking and moving that he feels in some way responsible for his aunt's death. From the time he zombie-walked into her line of vision early that morning, into the late afternoon, she has been sitting with him mostly in silence.

After seeing how peculiar Trais has been acting for the last several hours, Charlotte's mother finally grows tired of his strangeness and says in a hushed tone, "Get that boy away from here. He's giving off an awful energy."

Charlotte begs and pleads with her mother to let Trais stay a while longer, so she can talk to him and help him figure out a plan, but her mother does not budge.

She says, "Charlotte, dear, he is on his way to his destiny. There's no amount of planning in the world that's gonna stop that. Let him go on."

Charlotte reluctantly stops pleading. She knows from the look in his face and how different he was just nine months ago that whatever has happened to Trais has changed him forever.

Charlotte says to her mother, "Mom, just let me walk him to the bus stop. I know his brother lives somewhere along the 20 Madison bus line. Just let me walk him to the bus and put him on it and maybe he'll make his way to his brother's place."

Before agreeing, her mother estimates the three-block walk, how much time it will take to get there and back, and explains to Charlotte how she has exactly thirty minutes to be back home.

After promising to return on time, Charlotte gaily walks arm-in-arm with Trais down the street.

§

Trais heard what Charlotte and her mother said. Their conversation heightened his already growing paranoia. A cold sweat trickles down his back. He shivers. The shivering causes him to shake and everyone around him knows something is deathly wrong. He mumbles to Charlotte, "I feel like something's after me."

Charlotte quickens her pace and says, "Trais, just relax, please go to your brother."

She reaches for his hand but he pulls it away. Being touched is not what he needs. Every brush of their hand reminds him of Eddie and he is repulsed to the point of vomiting by the connection to that and his aunt's death.

Again, her hand comes in contact with his and immediately hot slimy water pours from his mouth. Charlotte looks at him lurch and heave, and when he finally belches air and wipes the tears from his eyes, she hands him napkins from her purse. Her only thought at this point is, *Lord, just let me get him to the bus stop.*

They finally arrive at their destination. Charlotte watches Trais. His head is drenched and he is pacing. The way he keeps rocking his head back and forth as if to communicate "no" is making her uneasy. He is becoming more unstable by the moment and she now finds herself desperately searching for the bus, so she can put him on it and be done with this matter. *C'mon 20*, she thinks. Just to calm her own anxiety, she closes her eyes to keep from being overwhelmed with his odd and ominous energy.

Before her eyes can rest, Trais mutters, "The bus is coming." Charlotte's eyes open and immediately focus on two imposing figures quickly advancing in their direction.

At first, she thought they were just hurrying for the bus, but then she saw their eyes locked on Trais as if he was their target. Two Black men, then three, were just milliseconds from her and Trais.

Charlotte does her best to hurry the unsuspecting Trais onto the bus. In an instant, she is pushed aside and Trais is in their grasp.

Charlotte watches as Trais with one foot on the stair of the bus and the other on the ground falls onto his back. The men's fists explode onto his face, chest, arms, and neck. As if in slow motion, she watches as the men's knees bend and their legs raise and the whites of their gym shoes kick Trais with combustion and cause his body to jump and jerk with great commotion.

"What are ya'll doing?! What is going on?!" Charlotte screams.

The sound of Charlotte's voice causes Trais to open his eyes. He listens as curses jet out from the men's mouths, crisscross, and flit through the air. Trais notices that one of the attackers looks vaguely familiar. He's the angriest of the three. He grabs Trais around the neck with his hands and pushes his fingers deep into his throat. His palms filled with the steam of anger loosen the breath from Trais's body.

"No, no!" Charlotte yells.

As Trais fades from consciousness he sees all the faces of the children he's touched. Their faces are stained with tears, their hearts beat loudly in their chests. In his spirit, Trais cries out to them, "I'm sorry. I didn't want to be what I was. I didn't want to be a pedophile."

Eons from Trais's mind, outside of his body, Charlotte screams, and the men continue beating him. The men's fists and feet against Trais's face make cracking, popping, flat, slapping sounds. Their punches, kicks, and grunts form a chord. Their shoes against his head, ribs, and shoulders rattle his organs.

Inside Trais's mind, among the faces of the children he had violated, two women appear. He remembered seeing them as a young child. They stared at him as he was on his way to school one day. They followed him for three blocks. Right before he entered the playground of the school, they handed him a pouch no larger than his six-year-old hand that had small rocks inside, a shell, and a piece of a feather. Afterward, they said nothing, walked away. He never saw them again.

He took the pouch home to his mother. She opened it, threw what she called the "junk" in the garbage and made the pouch her change purse. He remembered feeling like he had lost something.

For the first time since that time, again they appear. Their spirits are dressed in their Sunday's best. They kneel down beside him and hold his hands. The mens' kicks and punches hit Trais, but pass through the women.

With a small voice one says, "Trais, if only you had listened, if only you had turned back all those times the Lord tried to reach you, this would not be. I plead with you, Trais, call on Him. Rebuke the power of that spirit in the lives of the children you hurt. Just ask and you will receive (Matthew 7:7-8). Ask the Lord to bind the demonic spirit that was unleashed onto you and that you passed onto those children."

With broken teeth and a swelling jaw, Trais moans, "Please heal Baby Eddie, Lord, please heal all the children I harmed.

In an instant, the face of a child Trais touched expands before him. The eyes are scarred with pain, and a mask of perversity covers it. Trais's body responds sexually to it. The kneeling women shake their heads, each releases his hand, fizzle, and disappear.

Trais's spirit panics, "Lord, please bless the families I have hurt and don't let the children I've touched do to others what I did to them."

In the earthly realm, Charlotte continues to scream a dreadful, deeply human, primal, incomprehensible combination of yelps and yells. Trais's attackers synchronize their movements. They stomp, tear, and pummel. With each connection to Trais's body, their fists get tighter, their feet kick harder. Kick, punch, slam, hit, kick, slap, punch. Trais knows this will be his final resting place.

Baby Eddie appears to Trais. Eddie prays for Trais's soul and asks the Lord to not let Trais's life be lived in vain.

The vision of Eddie is then replaced, Trais sees the men who are beating him; their skin flashes: muscles, blood, organs, bones, veins, then skin again; on their veins processions of women, men, and children scream; in their blood, people of every color cry out tormented by the same pedophilic spirit that ravaged Trais's life. All of them cry out in languages known and unknown.

The angriest of the men beating Trais becomes an angel, who is both man and woman, infant and child. In the angel's hand is a great rope with a noose on one end and a millstone for each child Trais abused on the other. As the noose places itself around Trais's neck, the angel says, "Your life was not lived in vain." Then, Trais's trinity, *Trais's trinity*—his desires, his body, and his fantasies—are thrown into the deepest part of a dark and roaring sea (Matthew 18:6), and Trais breathes his last breath.

13

Oakland lowered then closed the book.

With a voice clear and proud and strong and determined, he said, "Those was the final days of my son's life."

All of the embarrassment Oakland felt earlier had been resolved. He rested in knowing that he had had the decency to be ashamed for not knowing his son, raising his son. And he rested in understanding that although his son died as a result of his choices to not correct his sexual thoughts and behavior involving children, his son's story would live on and would be used to help others.

Queena, Unice, and BarLee stared at Oakland, breathless. BarLee asked Oakland, "How did you read straight through like that? I wanted to stop you so many times and ask if you were okay, if you needed a break."

Oakland said, while looking at the sun setting around them, "There wasn't time for a break. There isn't time for breaks anymore. I have to tell people the lessons of my son's tragic life. I have to be his parent now. I have to do right by him. I have to move him from anti-hero to hero by sharing his hardships with others, by allowing his truth to encourage others to do the right thing, so that their lives do not end like his did, overcome and undone by perversity."

Queena sighed deeply. She thought of her mother, and all the boys— neighborhood boys, boys she had gone to school with—who had been with her mother. She thought of the boys, the really young ones, who would come over with their older brothers and fathers, and how the older ones thought it was funny when they'd make the young boys smack her mother on the butt or kiss her with open mouths. She cried as she thought of all the adults who thought exposing their children, especially their boys, to sex was funny and cool.

Queena remembered the men who said, "He gon' do it anyway. I'm just showing him how to do it right;" and the women who told their daughters, "if you gon' be a hoe, be a good one." At that moment, Queena stood up, held her hands in the air and yelled, "I surrender! I don't want that life, Lord."

Oakland, BarLee, and Unice were confused.

Queena looked at Oakland and said, "I will help you. I cannot watch all the bad stuff I've seen happen anymore. I'm broken. The so-called adults in my life done abused me, took the parts of me they wanted and left the rest. Trais is no different than me. I just haven't done what he did yet."

Queena stopped looking at Oakland and looked to heaven, "If I go back to that life...that will be my life. I'll be next. I rebuke that life, Lord, please forgive me for my thoughts and my actions. I repent!"

Unice stood and hugged Queena.

BarLee walked over to Queena and said, "Well, it's been confirmed. I have two daughters now."

Oakland with his hand on BarLee's shoulder said, "And, brother, now I have two nieces to help you protect and watch over."

With the sun precisely at its sunset position, just peeking over the horizon, Queena, Unice, Oakland, and BarLee prayed with their hands clasped together. They asked God for victory over fear, triumph over harsh judgment, and strength for the fight. They petitioned their Heavenly Father to help those who struggle with sexual attractions and practices that destroy.

They each said, with Oakland leading, "Father in Heaven, use us and Trais's story as instruments of Your grace; empower us in Your name to be useful in the transformation of souls troubled with pedophilic desires."

Part Four

A Closing Message from the Author

Reader, thank you for your time. I hope reading *Traces* was an enriching and enlightening experience that has prompted you to consider even more carefully the plight of those who have been abused and have become abusers.

For those of you who know someone who is struggling with being attracted to children, please encourage them to get help and to read books that directly examines the topic without sexualizing the subject, eroticizing the matter, or condemning the perpetrator of such acts without any mention of recourse. In addition to that, please pray for those who are burdened with visitations from the demonic forces that cause such thoughts and behavior.

And for those of you who are fighting the battle, I do believe that faith in, and obedience to, Christ will position you to receive Holy Ghost power, which is the only spiritual force that can overcome such strongholds.

For you, dear, who are stricken and suffering, I stand in agreement with you as you surrender your will to our Heavenly Father and pray for healing while demonstrating your faith through corrected actions. I pray that you see your situation through spiritual eyes that are under the power of the Holy Spirit, and that you acknowledge your pain, the pain of others, and the life-strangling problems that sexual abuse really causes. I pray that you have renewed empathy and that your heart breaks for children instead of devouring them. I pray that you repent of your sins. I pray for your soul.

As you begin your new life in recovery, please remember to pray for yourself, fast for your recovery, and hold on to God while you let go of those things that are actively seeking to destroy you.

Notes

_____

_____

_____

_____

_____

_____

_____

_____

_____

CPSIA information can be obtained at www.ICGtesting.com
Printed in the USA
LVOW11s1855130516

488143LV00007B/540/P